# RUTHLESS BETRAYAL

## DARK ENEMIES BOOK TWO

### ZOE DELANEY

# AUTHOR'S NOTE

This is a *dark* Mafia romantic suspense book, and as such, there will be triggers for some readers, including kidnapping, forced proximity, dubious consent, use of guns, death, mention of torture, possible PTSD, and a morally gray hero and heroine. This book and series are suitable for readers 18+.

*To my readers, first and foremost—thank you. Without readers, this series would not have come to life and I am grateful for each and every one of you.*

*To my amazing family and friends who believe in my writing and cheer me on even in my darkest moments—thank you.*

*To my sister Sandra, who is the best at brainstorming ideas and helped me rework a couple of plot points to make this book even stronger—thank you.*

*"Run, my dear, from anything
That may not strengthen
Your precious budding wings."*
Hafez

*Aria*

I WAS BREE, once upon a time. Then a monster kidnapped me, and I was reinvented as Bianca Carlotti-Agosti, a mob boss's wife.

Today I answer to the name Aria, and I live a life as far removed from Boston high society as possible.

Though I know in my heart Bianca still lives. Buried deep, but she's there. Holding a candle to my past in the darkness inside my sick and ravaged soul.

"Mrs. Lowe? *Hello*? Aria Lowe?"

The impatience in the receptionist's tone indicates she must have been calling my name for some time.

I jump to my feet and immediately sway as dizziness hits. *Whoa.* I reach out blindly and feel the comforting hands of someone on my arm, my back. Steadying me.

"Careful, love. Blood pressure is all over the place during pregnancy."

I blink and focus on the woman next to me. Another patient by the look of her belly, which is even more swollen than mine. I'm more than six months along now. She must be almost ready to give birth. She grins at me and releases my arm when I smile back.

"I should know," she adds in a wry tone. "This is my fourth."

"Wow. Congratulations. And thank you." My manner remains reserved, though I'm grateful for her assistance. I'm not used to socializing with people these days. Even this short exchange fills me with anxiety.

*Don't be stupid.* It's a pro-bono-style obstetrics clinic in downtown Cleveland, held once a fortnight for those who can't afford a more standard level of health care. Or those who can't afford for their personal details to be added to the proper health care system.

Those like me.

On the run from my mob boss husband *and* the Feds who want to convict him.

It's not Canada, the place to which I intended to run. Not by a long shot. But Cleveland was where the bus was headed the day I arrived in Augusta. I jumped off one bus and looked for the first one out of there. And somehow, when I arrived here, I finally felt safe.

For the first time in months, I felt like no one was watching me. I could breathe at last.

This city is not the place I am likely to run into anyone from my old way of life. Nor is this clinic.

*Don't be anxious*, I tell myself. It's not good for the baby.

"I'm Nita," the woman says, indicating the receptionist, who is now scowling my way. "I've seen you here before. Better go before you lose your spot in the queue."

"Oh, yes. She doesn't look happy." I start toward the desk, but then impulse stays me.

I turn back to Nita. She's older than my twenty-five years, perhaps by ten years or so, but her eyes are kind, and she seems almost motherly in her manner.

How nice it would be to have a kind presence in my life. How nice to have *any* presence in my life. The loneliness of my current existence is almost crippling.

I open my mouth to suggest we go for a coffee after our appointments are done—though in truth, it would be tea rather than coffee as I can't face the taste of coffee at present—but in the end, I don't say anything. I simply shoot her another quick smile and head off to my appointment.

The last time I had friends, my husband's goons shot them.

I can't afford to get close to anyone anymore, no matter how lonely I feel. I couldn't bear it if I was the cause of anyone else getting hurt.

Or killed.

And I can't afford to let slip anything about who I was or where I'm from. Because being dragged back to face Rio Agosti would likely kill me, body and soul.

I've betrayed the man I love. My husband. A monster.

But he's coming for me; I feel it in my bones.

And even if I somehow survive the deadly punishment that I know he will mete out for my betrayal, I will *not* allow my child to be brought up in that way of life.

I will *die* before I hand over my baby to my husband.

———

MY FURNISHED ONE-BED apartment in Clark-Fulton is small and about as basic as it gets, but at least the space is clean, and the building occupants are quiet most of the time. The rent is cheap, and the landlord was willing to take advance payment for three months ahead. So, I know I have stability for a little while.

Stability, and a safe place where Rio has little chance of finding me.

Though my husband's connections are extensive, I can't imagine there'd be anything in this neighborhood that would warrant his attention and, if I keep my head down and don't engage with other people, I should be safe enough. I hope.

The Feds are another matter. They're probably looking for me too, not to arrest me but to use me to bring down Rio. I refuse to help them do that.

I may have run from him. I may be terrified of the consequences if he finds me. But he stole my heart, and I will never give him up in that way.

I used the fake ID that Carlos Rossi arranged for me to find this apartment and register at the nearby ob-gyn clinic only a couple of bus stops away. But everything else is on a cash-only basis, and I never leave home without my wig and contact lenses in place.

About a week ago, I saw someone hanging around as I came out of the apartment building, and he set my senses on alert. The guy didn't look like one of my husband's goons. He wasn't suited up, and he didn't have that hard, emotionless expression that I got used to back in Boston.

But there was something about him... The way he was simply loitering on the opposite side of the street with no purpose that I could discern. The speed with which he turned and began to walk away after I briefly met his gaze. But he didn't look back, and once he disappeared around the corner, my spidey senses began to calm.

Just a random dude. Nothing to worry about. I haven't seen him since, and I am beginning to feel slightly more settled, despite the aching loneliness.

I suppose I should feel guilty that I took the money and ID documents Carlos Rossi gave me to set up in Augusta. He said he had an apartment ready and a crew on the ground who were going to assist in establishing my new life there. Surprisingly, I don't feel too much guilt.

Rossi may not have been the one pulling the trigger that day in Rio's club when all those people died, but Anders, the man who led the attack, was Rossi's right hand—his *consigliere* they call it in that world.

Just like Danelli is Rio's second. And as much as Rossi protested that he knew nothing about the attack on Rio, part of me doesn't believe him. Danelli would never be able to do anything without Rio knowing about it.

So, Rossi is either a liar, or his hold on his family is loosening. And my understanding from the brief time I lived in that world is that either or both of those options are intensely dangerous.

Whether liar or weakling, Rossi's hands are tainted with blood as much as any of them.

I want none of it. And one day, when my new life is fully

established and I find a job, I intend to pay Rossi back. Anonymously, of course. But I do not want to be beholden to Rossi, any more than I do to Rio.

I'm doing this for my baby. A new life. A new start. Away from the long shadow of Mafia life—and death.

And even though I cry myself to sleep every night, craving Rio's touch, his strength, his energy, no one else ever needs to know about that.

The next time I attend the obstetrics clinic, Nita is there in the waiting area. This time, she grins and pats the seat next to her as I enter. "Come sit with me, Aria. Let's chat."

My heart leaps. Other than a couple of neighbors who wave but don't stop to speak, and the kid at the local grocery store where I get my food, I haven't spoken with anyone since the last time I was here two weeks ago. The thought of *chatting*, as Nita calls it, is both energizing and nerve-racking.

*Don't trust anyone. Don't share anything that may get back to Rio.*

Tentatively, I take the seat beside her. "Thanks, Nita. How are you feeling?"

I rub my expanding belly. I'm only just heading into my final trimester. Nita looks like she's nearing the end of her pregnancy and shifts in her chair as if trying and failing to find a comfortable position.

I expect that will be me in another month or two.

"A bit more sleep would be good, but that's never gonna happen with three other kids in the house. All under five, too."

I raise my brows. "Seriously? How do you manage? I hope your husband..." I trail off awkwardly, aware that I'm

6

making assumptions about her life. "Sorry. Don't mean to pry."

I don't want to encourage questions about my life. My secrets. I imagine how that may go. *My husband? Oh, he's a mob boss who's probably going to kill me when he finds me. That's if the Feds don't find me first.*

That likely wouldn't go down too well as an opening move toward friendship. I study Nita's expression, tired but still sporting a friendly smile and a sparkle in her eyes. Do I want to be friends with her? Is it possible to make connections here, without endangering myself or my baby? Or her?

"I don't have a husband," she says easily. She doesn't seem upset that I've asked, simply gives a philosophical shrug. "He ran off as soon as I told him about this one." She pats her stomach, and her smile dips. "Thank God. I hope he never comes back."

"Oh. Well," I mumble, not sure how to respond.

How bad must it have been for her to be happy that she's about to have her fourth child without the support of a partner?

She laughs, a light tinkling sound that causes my lips to lift into an involuntary smile. "Don't look so sad. *I'm* not! Wanna have a drink after our appointments?"

"Um..."

"Oh, you know, not a *drink* drink. Like, a coffee or something, is what I meant. When I'm not heavily pregnant, I usually work in a diner not far from here. I still get a staff discount."

Her hopeful gaze pins me, and suddenly I'm tired of being alone. Adrift among a sea of complete strangers with no one to talk to. Being disengaged really fucking sucks.

*Rio will never know. He can't hurt her like he did Dave and Shelley. It'll be okay.* "Sure. I'd love that, Nita. Thanks."

The receptionist calls her name at that point, and she hauls up awkwardly to her feet.

"Great. I'll hang out here after and wait for you. See you then."

As Nita wobbles off for her appointment, I pray I haven't just made the biggest mistake of my life. For me. Or for her.

## 2

---

*"I am, indeed, a king, because I know how to rule myself."*
Pietro Aretino

*Aria*

THE DINER NITA steers me to is only a block up from the clinic. When we're finally inside and seated in a corner booth, she spears me with a curious look. "You in some kind of danger, Aria?"

"What? Why would you ask…"

She grins. "You kept looking over your shoulder as we walked—well, waddled I guess is the more accurate term—here. You're still checking our surroundings even now. And you took *that* seat, which gives you a great view of the door and everyone who comes in here."

Heat blooms in my cheeks. Checking for danger has

become such a habit in the few months since I escaped from Rio that I hadn't realized I was doing that today.

I can't tell her the truth, but I need to give her something. It seems like forever since I had real friends, but I still remember how it's supposed to work. Give and take.

"Yeah, I… err… I don't want my ex to find out where I live. He's…" *Complex. Dangerous. Sexy as fuck and easily the scariest person I've ever met.* I settle for, "Problematic."

Her gaze is wise as she searches my face. Then she nods. "All good, hon. Everyone has secrets from their past in this part of town."

I wonder what she means, and I'm about to ask when the server arrives with a pot of coffee. Nita accepts, but I shake my head.

"Could I please have tea instead?"

"And pie," Nita adds. "Two slices of your apple pie. Thanks, June. With a side of ice cream for each of us." She grins at me again. "My treat."

"Oh no, I—"

"I insist," Nita says firmly, as the server disappears behind the counter. "Staff discount, remember? I might be a single mom, but I'm good for it. And besides, you look as if you haven't had a good meal in a while."

I hate to admit it, but she's right. I've only got the funds Carlos gave me for my new start, and I need to make them last as long as I can. I've been living frugally, and a slice of warm apple pie paid for by a generous soul sounds like heaven right about now.

"Then thank you," I say, warmth spreading through me.

I've forgotten how nice it is to have someone in my life who cares. My dad is probably still off adventuring in the wilds of Asia somewhere. I figure I'll reach out to him around the time of my birthday so he doesn't worry when he can't get me on my old number, but that's another three months or so away.

I'm actually due to give birth close to the date of my birthday. I hope the baby doesn't come on my actual birthday though, given that is now also the anniversary of being snatched off the street by Rio.

"I promise to enjoy my pie and ice cream wholeheartedly," I say.

We laugh together, and in that moment, a kernel of hope blooms in my chest. Maybe it will be possible to make this new life work. Maybe it is possible to put the past behind me, and one day I may even have the chance to go back and see my old friends and work colleagues and explain what happened in more detail. Apologize for ruining their lives.

But even after the delicious pie and hot tea begin to fill my belly and calm my usually jangled nerves, I still glance up every time the bell rings above the door, studying who enters to see if I recognize a face. Or a hardened look.

And the fear still sits inside me. It's just tucked deeper down than before. Because I know Rio Agosti almost as well as I know myself. And he will never give up looking for me until the day he takes his last breath. I was his possession, and I betrayed him when I ran. An act I am sure he will never, ever forgive.

As much as I hope otherwise, it is really only a matter of time before he catches up with me, ready to mete out the punishment he thinks I deserve. I have no doubt that punishment will be severe. I only hope he spares our beautiful baby before he does so.

## Rio

I REACH the end of the terrace rooftop pool and turn in the water, starting another lap back the same way I've just swum. I do this every morning, over and over, back and forth, the laps serving both as exercise and distraction.

It has been over three months, and they haven't found her.

Since the massacre at the estate and the loss of my Aunt Francine, I can't bring myself to spend any length of time there. Everything is pristine, of course, and new security installed, but instead, I spend most of my days—and nights —here in my penthouse above the club. Working, swimming, and plotting revenge against those who harmed my family.

Against my wife, who stole my heart and then my child.

I will have my revenge on my enemies, and that revenge will be the sweetest thing of all.

So far, Danelli and his crew have scoured every possible lead for traces of Bianca. The private investigation firm I hired, Dartside Investigations, traced her to Augusta and then lost her. I even ordered the firm to put out feelers into Thailand, to track down her father and confirm she has had no contact with him.

Her adoptive father, that is. Her birth father—along with the rest of the Carlotti family—are long dead. As far as I've been able to ascertain over the years, Bianca is the last of her bloodline. At least, until our baby is born.

Familiar rage burns through my veins at the thought of my child being snatched out from under my nose. Granted, Bianca could not yet have had the child, but I need her back under my watchful gaze before that happens. I will never give up looking until she and my child—the heir to both the

Carlotti and the Agosti empires—are back in their rightful place.

By my side.

Only this time, she will bow to my will and obey me. And she will never escape me again.

I allowed her into my life, into my *heart*, and in return, she shredded the love and trust I bestowed and threw it in my face in the form of a million jagged shards.

I will not make that same mistake twice.

I reach the other end of the heated pool and prepare to turn yet again, but pause when one of my men approaches. I can tell from his gait that he has news. His steps are hurried, his breathing rough, and his hand clenches and unclenches around his cell phone as if he is both excited and afraid to pass on what he knows.

He *should* be afraid. My mood these days is…shall we say, fickle? And I am not in the frame of mind for anything other than good news.

I point to a stack of white towels on top of the cabinet near the wall, and he deviates from his path to grab one and then rushes over to hand it to me. I take my time, rubbing my face dry, trying to control my urge to reach up, grab him by the lapels of his suit jacket, and haul him down into the water. Venting my ever-present rage on the messenger will not achieve anything except a momentary sense of satisfaction.

When my emotions are under control, I toss the towel to one side and pin him with a stare. "Yes?"

The man's Adam's apple bobs as he swallows nervously, and my inner beast purrs. I like the fear I instil in others. It affirms the power I wield over my empire.

"I think we might have found her, Boss."

Whatever I expected from him, it is not those words. At

most, I expected a new lead. A new city to start scouring. I blink a couple of times to hide my shock, ducking down into the water and drifting backwards for a beat or two. Then I turn and make my way to the stepladder at the side of the pool, taking my time while I climb out and head over to reach for another pristine white towel.

Only when I have one towel draped over my shoulders and another around my hips do I turn and look at the messenger. His face is pale, his eyes glittering with excitement. He knows how much this means to me, and I hate that he knows.

My mouth thins. "By *her*, you mean…"

"Yes, sir. Bia… I mean… Mrs. Agosti. Your wife. I think we've found your wife."

"Where?"

"Cleveland, Boss."

The location does not compute. It seems so random; senseless almost. I can understand her crossing the border into Canada, or heading south or over toward the West Coast. Even disappearing into a nearby city like New York with its endless opportunities to hide among the populace.

"And you know this…how?"

"The firm you hired got a tip-off about a fake name she may have used. I'm not sure where the tip came from. They sent someone out to investigate and wanted confirmation they had the right woman before taking any action. They sent this."

When he holds out his cell for me to view, his hand trembles so hard I can barely focus on the screen. No matter. I recognize the contents of the photo on display. A matching set of rings—engagement and wedding—sit on what looks like a cheap bathroom countertop. I placed those rings on Bianca's long and delicate finger at our wedding several months ago.

My heart jolts, the faster-than-usual tick pounding all the way up into my throat. I adjust the towel around my neck.

*She kept her wedding ring set. Why would she keep her rings?*

Of all the places I thought my men would find her, Cleveland was not on the list of possibilities.

"Yes." I give the messenger a curt nod. "They are hers. Get me Danelli. I want him in my office in one hour."

"Yes, sir." He scurries off to do my bidding, already dialling a number on his cell as he rushes toward the roof terrace exit.

I raise my chin, tilting back my head and closing my eyes. The heat of the day will likely kick in soon. Summer in Boston can be hot and cloying, but up here on the roof terrace, above the constant bustle of the city below, the early morning breeze still holds a pleasant hint of coolness.

Thoughts whirl as I catalogue options for action. My wife will be brought back within days. Hours, if I have my way. And I always do. Then the fun will begin.

Excitement pools in my belly. The excitement of a successful hunt.

*Bianca, my love. My betrayer. You will not get away from me again.*

## 3

*"If you are swept off your feet, it's time to get on your knees."*
Fred Beck

*Aria*

FOR THE FIRST time since I arrived in Cleveland, happiness settles my mind. *I am safe.* The mantra repeats over and over in my head as Nita and I share stories about the discomfort of being pregnant, and our hopes and dreams for our new babies once they arrive in this world.

She's having a boy. She found out at one of her scans, but I've chosen not to find out. It seems more exciting that way. And it isn't like I have the budget to go out and get a bunch of blue- or pink-themed baby goods.

*I am safe. My baby is safe. We will survive this.*

And now I have a new friend to help stave off the loneliness.

Laughing with Nita over apple pie and ice cream felt unfamiliar, but there is a lightness in my thoughts and a bounce in my step as I head back to my apartment. I lift my face to enjoy the warmth of the afternoon sun. When I enter my building, I feel hopeful for the first time in a long time.

Life as I knew it before Rio is long gone. My life as Rio's wife—even though I know he loved me and I feel as if I will never breathe properly again without him—is over.

It is time to move on. And maybe my friendship with Nita will help me do that. Our next obstetric appointments are lined up to match, one after the other, and she has suggested we go for a walk at a nearby park afterward, providing it isn't too hot.

My steps are light on the stairs. My apartment is up two flights, and I usually drag my feet, clinging on the handrail and huffing and puffing. Today the ascent is easy. I hadn't realized how much my fear and sadness had weighed me down.

It isn't until I reach my landing that I pause. My neighbor is at his door, talking to a tall and very imposing-looking cop. Both of them turn to face me as I hover there, and my heart takes a jolt and lifts right up into my throat.

Is the cop here because of me?

"Hey, Aria," my neighbor calls out, dragging me into whatever it is whether I like it or not. "You had anything go missing recently? A few of us've been broken into." He glances at the cop. "She lives there." He points at my apartment door, and I proceed closer, trying to slow my racing heart.

Break-ins are not uncommon in this neighborhood. It's nothing. It has to be nothing. Not everything bad has to do with Rio or the men who work for him.

"You've had a break-in, Rick?" I ask, annoyed that my voice sounds so thin and reedy.

My neighbor nods and flashes me a lopsided grin. "Yeah. Lucky I ain't got nothin' too valuable. They got a couple of small things, but prob'ly gave up quick when they saw the shit in my place."

"Ma'am." The cop steps forward and introduces himself as Officer Howard. "Have you noticed anything out of the ordinary, Miss…"

He raises a brow, inviting me to provide my name, and a sudden sick dread passes through me.

What if the Feds are still looking for me, too? What if there's somehow a link somewhere, between Aria Lowe and Bianca Carlotti, or even Bree Walker, the girl I used to be? What if I give him my name and he figures out who I am and calls it in?

I swallow hard, and the cop's eyes narrow as he studies me. I'm making him wary with my hesitation.

I offer him a fake smile and my fake name. "I haven't seen anything untoward, Officer. I'm sorry." I glance at my door. "Should I check inside, just in case…"

"Yes. Do that," the cop says smoothly.

Too smoothly? Is he suspicious of me?

It takes a couple of tries to get my key into the lock. My hands are shaking just a little bit too hard. But at least the door's still locked and, when I enter, the apartment looks just as I left it.

Not that there's much here to steal, but there is a small TV and sound system which would be easy to grab. It still sits atop the corner entertainment unit.

"Looks okay," I confirm, the relief in my tone probably

evident to the cop standing in the doorway scanning the room.

I point to the intact entertainment equipment, and the cop gives a short nod. Then I wander into the tiny bedroom and through into the bathroom, more to be thorough than because there's anything valuable in either of those spaces for a thief.

I stop short.

Adrenaline lurches up through my body in a sudden violent rush. I clutch at the doorframe to avoid falling to the floor, and only just hold back a sob of terror.

There on the countertop, sitting neatly side by side, are my wedding and engagement rings. The rings I've kept hidden away in an unneeded tampon box at the back of my bathroom drawer ever since I arrived here. The rings I vowed to never lay eyes on again, unless I become desperate and need to pawn them.

The beautiful, ostentatious rings that Rio placed on my finger the day I became his wife and promised in front of a crowd of strangers to love, honor, and obey him.

The rings that became a symbol of my captivity and bound me to him and his violent world. Irrevocably, and forever.

---

*Aria/Bianca*

I HAVE no idea how I manage to stagger back out into the hallway and act as if everything is normal in front of Rick and the visiting police officer.

Somehow, I smile and nod and talk, and eventually the cop leaves, seeming satisfied, but I have no idea what was actually said, nor how I ended up back inside my apartment, door firmly closed, and with me sitting on the floor with my arms wrapped around my knees.

*He's found me.* He'll be sending his goons to fetch me soon enough. Will they shoot again, the way they did last time? Will innocent people around me die?

I rock back and forth, knowing I have to run. Knowing that my budding friendship with Nita will fall by the wayside because I won't even have the chance to say goodbye. Just like before, when Dave and Shelley got shot, and I disappeared out of their lives as if I'd never cared for them *or* my job at the rescue center.

I hate with all my being that this is now my life and that Rio has forced me into this.

I hate most of all that the monster haunting the shadows of my life is the father of my child. And that I can no more switch off from loving him than I can stop breathing.

*Hatred and love*, he said once, *are two sides of the same coin.* He was correct. Rio is my life, and he will likely herald my death.

I stop rocking and lay my hands over my swollen abdomen. *Little one, I promise that I will do everything I can to try and keep you safe.*

The thought of protecting my child galvanizes me into action. I lurch up to my feet and rush around the apartment, grabbing my backpack out from the shelf at the top of my wardrobe. Most of the belongings here are not mine—they came with the apartment, which was rented fully furnished. So, it only takes a few minutes to shove my meager collection of clothing, cash, and toiletries into my bag.

Adrenaline fuels my movements, and my limbs tremble, but I can't afford to waste another minute. He'll be here soon.

Or at least, his men will be. And I can only imagine what instructions they may have been given.

I betrayed a Mafia boss. I may still be his wife, but in their world, I probably deserve to die.

Finally, the rings sitting on the counter are the only items left of mine. I study them for several seconds, tempted to leave them as a sign to Rio's men when they come for me. A sign that I don't care about him or our marriage. A *fuck-you* message that he will receive loud and clear.

But that would be a lie. And when I raise my gaze to my haunted reflection in the mirror above the sink, I read the truth in my stricken expression.

Of course I care. I care *desperately*. If he agreed to give up the Mafia life, I would run back to him in a heartbeat.

But he won't. He can't. I don't need to ask him the impossible, as I *know* him. The life into which he was born is part of his blood. The death and violence may taint his soul, but it is part of who he is.

I grab for the rings and shove them deep down in my backpack, trying to ignore the traitorous voice inside my head that taunts, "But you were born to that life too, Bianca. Your blood—your soul—is as dark and tainted as his."

One last look around the small space that has been my home for the past three or so months, and I tug at the door, half expecting to see Rio's goons already in the hallway.

*Don't be stupid*, I tell myself. Whoever was here needs time to get the message to Rio, and then he'll need time to arrange a team to head here and... And do what? Kill me? Kidnap me yet again? Hurt me, as I surely must have hurt him?

I have no idea what he may have planned for me. But they'll have to catch me first.

21

I'm sure he doesn't have anyone already on the ground here in Cleveland—his reach can't possibly be everywhere, and I don't see why this city would be on his radar at all.

I have time to get away. I'm sure of it.

I rush for the stairs, tripping halfway down the last flight in my haste. I clutch at the handrail to steady myself and proceed more sedately down to the first level. I cannot afford a twisted ankle, or worse, any harm to come to my baby if I fall.

*Slow and steady, Aria.* I chant the words in my head, over and over, like a calming incantation. *Slow and steady, one foot in the front of the other, and soon, you will be hidden away once more.*

I reach the street and look both ways for signs of pursuit before I start toward the nearest bus stop, only a few doors down from my building. No dark sedan or town car in sight. No goons in suits. Not yet, anyway.

I figure I'll take the first bus that comes along, and then decide what to do next once I'm on my way. I'll have to give up the name Aria Lowe, of course. He will have that information by now, given they found my place and broke in.

I'm so tired of changing my name. Tired of trying to reinvent myself, when all I wanted less than a year ago was to head out and enjoy my twenty-fifth birthday by celebrating with an espresso martini.

That seems so long ago now. A lifetime. More than that, even.

I fought to keep Bree Walker, but in the end, I accepted that Bianca Carlotti was my destiny; my birthright. The name Aria is useful, and I wish I *was* her, but I'm not. It won't matter what I call myself, now or any time in the future.

Bianca Carlotti-Agosti is who I will always be, deep down inside, whether I want to be her or not.

I'm studying the timetable on the side of the bus stop, trying to work out whether to wait here or leave this area on foot and find somewhere else from which to catch my next bus to nowhere, when the purr of an engine behind me jerks my heart rate almost to a stop.

Ordinary cars don't sound so smooth, so powerful.

Slowly, I turn, knowing what I'll see before the truth materializes in front of my eyes.

A large black limousine glides to a stop beside me, and I want to scream and scream and scream because I know exactly what it means. But when I open my mouth, nothing comes out except a tiny whimper.

Until the rear door opens, and one black-trouser-clad leg emerges, followed by another. When the large-framed man emerges and unfolds to his full height, I gape at the apparition before me. My previous whimper turns into a moan.

Because this is not one of Rio's goons. It is not Danelli, Rio's second, who I've been watching for over my shoulder ever since I ran.

Standing in front of me, staring down with the coldest expression I have ever seen on any human being, is Rio Agosti himself.

He came for me. Personally.

My husband, here in person to exact vengeance on the woman who betrayed him. And I can do nothing except continue to stare up at him, because every part of my body is frozen in place with terror.

4

---

*"The most common way people give up their power is by thinking they don't have any."*
Alice Walker

*Rio*

HER HAIR and eyes are different, but I would know my wife anywhere. Her very presence energizes me like no one else, and no amount of wigs or colored contact lenses can hide her from me.

She is thinner than I remember, notwithstanding the pregnant belly, of course. But her cheekbones stand out, her jawline is more sharply delineated, and her cheeks are pale. Too pale. Those signs tell me she hasn't been looking after herself as well as she could. As well as she should, when she's carrying the Agosti heir.

Her eyes are enormous in her face, dark circles surrounding them that should make her look older, more tired. But instead, she just seems…fragile. Delicate. Not what I was expecting.

But the defiance in her tight expression and the fire in her eyes—even though they are fake blue, not her usual honey brown—are as intense as I remember from before. And instantly, my body tightens in unwanted arousal.

*Fuck.* I did not expect she would still have that much of an effect on me.

I do not *want* to feel anything for this woman except cold, hard anger.

When I called Danelli into my office, I had every intention of ordering him onto my private jet to head here on my behalf. The words that came out of my mouth shocked my second, but they shocked me even more.

"Ready the jet. I'm going to collect my wife."

"Wait, Boss, I don't think you…" He swallowed down whatever else he planned to say after I pinned him with a stare, and nodded instead. "Yes, sir. I'll make the calls."

I don't know why I'm here. Like an errand boy. A messenger. I should have let Danelli come in my place. Me being here sends the wrong message to everyone. It makes me appear lovestruck. Pathetic.

I should be the hunter *stalking* my prey, not chasing after it like a puppy.

But here I am, and here she is, and I want to simultaneously lay her over my lap and spank the living daylights out of her, or fold her into my embrace and never let her go.

*Weak.* She makes me weak.

"Get in the car. And then remove the wig and contacts." My tone is icy.

Good. At least I have some semblance of control left when it comes to her. Even if only my voice.

I step to one side and gesture her in, but instead of immediately complying, she takes a tiny step backward. Still thinking of running, even when she knows the act is impossible.

"How did you find me?" Her voice floats between us, a mere whisper, but my senses are so tuned in to her that I pick up other nuances in her tone.

She is terrified, and at the same time, she's furious, but there is something else running beneath the words—not relief, exactly. I can't pinpoint what it is. If I didn't know better, I'd guess an element of desire. But that cannot be. She would never have run in the first place if desire still lived in her heart.

And yet, it is that unknown and indefinable element that excites my blood in a way I can't explain.

"Rossi led us to Augusta and gave us your fake name." Even with that lead, the investigators lost her trail after that, until a fortuitous stroke of luck.

"Carlos Rossi? But he... Why would he..."

She frowns, and I grin at her obvious confusion, though the lack of humor in my expression must be clear because she recoils from the smile.

"Yes. He thought twice about helping you, Bianca, especially when you didn't arrive at the lovely little home he had arranged for you. He decided in the end he would rather give you up than face my wrath when I discovered what he had done."

"Is he... Did you..." Her hand flutters at her throat as if she can't articulate her query.

"Did I kill him?" *I wanted to, little bird.* I came so close that I held the gun to his head and only stayed the action when he begged for his life.

I gesture again, and this time, she climbs into the rear compartment of the limousine without protest. When we are both seated, with her facing the front opposite me, I rap my knuckles on the partition behind my head to signal the driver to move. She does what I've ordered and removes the wig and contact lenses, then ruffles a hand through her hair, loosening her own slightly sweaty locks. I study her closely, wanting to gauge her reaction to my next words.

"Rossi showed a modicum of sense in coming to me, and after begging for his life, he provided information regarding a rival who may have been involved in action against my family. I have, therefore, spared him. For now. Except for one of his fingers. I did not spare him that."

She gasps. "His...*finger*? You cut off..."

She opens and closes her mouth a couple of times, as if she plans to add something else and then changes her mind.

My inner monster enjoys her shock. *Yes, little bird. This is who you have betrayed.*

"But it is not Carlos Rossi to whom you owe my visit today. *Your* betrayer is a little closer to home than that."

"My betrayer? What do you mean?"

I lean forward, deliberately pushing into her space, noting the flicker of her eyes. She is as aware of me in a physical sense as I am of her.

"I mean, my dear Bianca, that *karma* is a bitch. You betrayed me, and in turn, your friend Nita betrayed *you*."

---

*Bianca*

27

"I DON'T BELIEVE YOU." That can't be true. Nita wouldn't do that.

But even as I fight the urge to lunge at him and slap his face for his evil lie, I know deep down that he's telling the truth.

He must be. How else could he possibly know about Nita?

Unless, of course, his goons have been stalking me for some time, and listened in on my coffee catch-up with her. But I was watching the door, and there was no one near enough to hear our conversation.

Ice fills my veins as a thought intrudes. "Is Nita okay? Don't hurt her. Please, she has nothing to do with your world. Your violent, sick world. She has kids."

One of Rio's brows rises, and his nose wrinkles slightly as if I'm merely a piece of garbage on the bottom of his shoe.

"My violent, sick world? Yes, it is violent. Yes, it may be sick at times. But it is not simply *my* world, Bianca. It is *ours*. You were born to the Mafia life, and our *world* runs in your very blood. Do not be so quick to judge."

He lifts his cell phone and taps the screen a few times, then holds it out to me. I don't want to look. I know that whatever he's trying to show me will be something bad. Something hurtful. But I can't stop my gaze from dropping to the screen.

I see a news article about prominent business people in Boston—"movers and shakers," the article calls them. And right there, decorating the article, is a photograph of Rio with me hanging off his arm. It must have been taken the night of the gala event where I first met the federal agent, Felicity. I recognize my dress and the background at the marina hotel.

"She saw this in her news feed and recognized you," Rio

says smoothly, while a sick feeling rises in my throat. "And then she called my office. Dana passed the message on to Danelli. Still don't believe me?"

"No," I whisper, but of course we both know I'm lying. His explanation rings of truth.

Dana is Rio's assistant, and I can imagine her excitement at receiving such a call and being able to please her boss with the news.

Like everyone who works for Rio, she adores him and fears him in equal measure.

I lean my head back against the seat and close my eyes, trying to block him out. How can this be happening? Is there nowhere safe from the reach of Rio Agosti?

"Here."

I open my eyes to see him holding out his phone again, only this time he has dialed a number, and the phone is actually ringing. When a woman answers, he puts the handset on speaker so we can both hear her more clearly.

"Hello? Who is this? Hello?" Nita's voice fills the space in the car.

I want to throw up all over Rio's lap, but instead, I simply say, "Nita. Why? *Why*?"

There's a sharp inhale at the other end, and then Nita answers in a voice filled with regret. "I'm so sorry, Aria. Or should I say, Bianca? But when I saw that photo and realized who you were, I..." She pauses, as if taking the time to choose her words carefully.

It doesn't matter what words she uses. Betrayal is betrayal.

"I had to think of my kids, Aria. Four under five, and their asshole dad is gone. I made light of it to you, but I can't do it, hon. Not on my own. I needed the money to help out, at least for a bit. I am truly sorry, you know."

"Sure. Whatever. I hope he paid you well. Goodbye." I lean forward and press the End button before Rio can do it, then shift along the seat until I'm as far away from my husband as I can be. I wrap my arms around my middle, fighting nausea.

The thing is, I can't even blame Nita. Not really. She just did exactly what I did. I betrayed Rio and ran from him to protect my child. She betrayed me for her children. She was just better at it than me.

Like Rio said, *karma*. It really is a bitch.

I release a laugh at the irony, then keep laughing, until the laughter turns to sobs, and I stuff a hand against my mouth in a vain attempt to stop the hysterical sounds from emerging.

He tucks away his phone, then sits quietly, studying me.

The quiet is worse than his raging temper. I can tell he is simmering with unspoken emotion, but the lack of expressiveness means I'm just waiting for the explosion. And the longer it doesn't come, the more difficult it gets to simply wait for the reaction.

Finally, I can't stand the silence any longer.

"Are we driving all the way back to Boston? And where in Boston are we going? Do you still live at the riverside estate, or do you have somewhere new you hang out?" *Since the massacre.* I don't voice the latter, but his eye twitches in the slightest possible tell.

The memory clearly still affects him. As it would. He lost his aunt in that attack on the estate, along with several employees.

"Well, Rio? I have a right to know what you're going to do with me."

"*You* believe you have rights? After your betrayal?"

There is no emotion in his tone. No light in his eyes. Maybe I made up all the softer feelings I thought he'd developed toward me in my brief time as his wife.

Or maybe those feelings were true, and I destroyed them when I ran. Maybe he was so unused to trusting anyone that when I betrayed that trust, everything human in him simply shrivelled up and died.

"Please, Rio. Are we driving back to Boston?"

The corner of his eye again tics briefly, before he rubs a finger over the area. The twitch disappears as if it never existed at all. "We will fly back. The airport isn't far."

His mouth snaps shut, as if even that brief explanation is too much for him to have revealed.

"Are you going to kill me, Rio?"

I don't mean for the question to come out so shakily, but every part of me is terrified about what I'm heading into.

He laughs, the sound brief and humorless. I press back into the leather of the seat, but there's nowhere to go.

"Not yet, little bird," he answers in a soft tone.

The softness is deceptive. I hear the underlying anger beneath it.

"You are carrying my child. When the baby is born, I will reconsider your future then."

"But—"

"No, Bianca. No but. No if. No maybe. Be quiet now. I have work to attend to."

He turns away from me, twisting his body so he is no longer facing me, and pushes a couple of buttons on the door beside him. A table rises up from the floor of the limo, and I shuffle my feet quickly to the side so they don't get caught up in the mechanism. The table holds a shiny silver laptop. He flips the lid and begins to tap on the keyboard, and the rest of our journey to the airport is conducted in silence.

I have so many unanswered questions, most of which I'm afraid to ask.

*Not yet*, he said. What does that mean? When my baby arrives, is he going to kill me and dump my body in the river behind his estate? Am I going to get the concrete-boots treatment that everyone in the movies talks about? Is that an actual thing in Rio's world?

*Of course it is*, my mind whispers. *You know what kind of world he inhabits.*

I can't seem to control my racing heart, and I take deep, gulping breaths, struggling to slow everything down and stop the fear coursing through my system. The breathing ploy doesn't work.

I don't know exactly what Rio has in store for me back in Boston, but I do know one thing. It will not be pleasant.

And quite possibly, it may prove deadly.

---

## 5

*"We're all captives of something, even things we don't want to admit to."*
Raven Kennedy, *Glint*

*Rio*

I WANT TO TOUCH HER. I want to shove aside this fucking laptop and drag her onto my lap. Remind her of what we had together. Before she ran. But that says more about me and my tenuous hold on control than it does about anything else, and lately, I feel I am hanging on to my power by my fingernails.

So, for now, I keep my hands on the keyboard and studiously ignore her while I pretend to study some reports sent through by my accounting team. Her scent fills the cabin of the limo, and I struggle not to be obvious when I inhale the citrus that permeates the air.

I missed her scent. I missed *her*.

My own wife running from me was one thing, but now I have her back, and she will not get away from me again.

Carlos Rossi and that mess with Anders is a whole other level of disaster.

Anders invaded my home. Killed my flesh and blood. Not on Rossi's behalf, perhaps, but definitely not working on his own. He had someone pulling his strings, and it is time I found out who and paid that person a visit.

Revenge is not a dish best served cold. When family is involved, revenge is best served up so hot it burns everything that touches it.

Whoever sent Anders is gunning for my family. For my business. For *me*.

Their message was loud and clear, and some are listening; wondering if I've lost my hold on Boston. I need to wrest back my control before an all-out war ensues.

Carlos Rossi disclosed some useful information about Anders, and that is the only reason he's not dead. For now, I need him alive so he can continue to feed me the information I require to retain my position at the head of the family.

Rossi's investigation discovered that Anders had switched allegiance to a new player in the field. No one has been able to ascertain who he is, where he came from, or where he is now, other than whispers of a first name. Anton. Or Antonio.

Danelli and my various teams are on the job, as is the private investigation firm I use from time to time. Nothing has come to light regarding anyone named Antonio or Anton, or various other derivatives of that name.

I flick a glance at Bianca, wondering if she knows anyone named Anton. I cannot believe she was anything other than a complete innocent when she was first brought to me. The background checks were too thorough to miss anything significant. As ludicrous as the idea is, though, I don't completely dismiss it. Her betrayal may only have occurred after we were married, when the federal agents at the gala event put the idea of bringing me down into her head.

But trust was destroyed the day she ran. And I don't know if she will ever earn it back.

Another email briefly takes my attention. There has been trouble at the wharf. Again. Third time in the past two months that one of our deliveries has been delayed in transit. My mouth tightens. The wharf is ours, key personnel bought and paid for longer than I can remember. Since my father's time, in fact. There should be no trouble with any of our deliveries, even if the Feds have decided to step up and make trouble.

I flag the message to be dealt with as soon as I return to my office and have a chance to speak privately with Danelli. In the meantime, I tap out a response to my lawyer, Carnarvon, telling him to look into the financial side of things and ensure nothing has changed in that regard.

Since Bianca ran, it feels as if I have been fighting spot fires at every turn. Each issue has been small and swiftly dealt with, but it is only a matter of time before someone decides to take another shot at dethroning the Agosti-Carlotti power base.

My thoughts inevitably turn back to the mystery man behind the hit that killed my aunt. I must find him. The man —whoever he is—struck at the heart of my family and my home. That must not go unpunished. If I allow that, then I deserve to lose my position.

That is the thing Bianca likely does not understand. Her act of defiance against me had the potential to weaken our hold on this city. Her attempt at freedom, coming so soon after the hit on my family, has meant I must tighten my grip on the business.

Publicly, and powerfully.

If I do not, then we risk an all-out turf war.

And unfortunately for my dear wife, she is the one who is about to suffer the consequences.

------

*Bianca*

RIO IGNORES me for most of the journey. The flight isn't long, but it feels like forever. I am placed in a seat at the opposite end of the cabin to him, and an attendant straps me in. As if I'm a child and cannot do it myself. Partway through the flight, my contrariness gets the better of me, and I stand and move to the leather seat opposite Rio, sitting down and staring at him in the hope of gaining his attention.

He looks up briefly, spears me with that intent chocolate-brown gaze, then waves a hand, and the attendant appears seemingly out of nowhere, gently taking my arm and urging me back to my designated seat.

Is this how it's going to be from now on? He's punishing me with the silent treatment?

It seems childish, and not what I expected from a man like him.

I half expect a dungeon and handcuffs. Not the fluffy, erotic kind either.

It isn't until we are back in Boston and inside yet another limousine, gliding through the city that I used to call home, that he deigns to speak once again.

"Why did you keep the rings?"

"I beg your pardon? I mean…are you referring to the wedding ring your men photographed? In my bathroom?"

His nod is short and sharp.

"Well, because…" Why *did* I keep them? Why did I take them in the first place? "I…"

*I love you, and I wanted a reminder of that love, even though what we had was twisted and toxic and unhealthy.*

"Because they're worth money, and I planned to hock them in the future when I needed to," I say.

I expect his expression to tighten, his eyes to spark with displeasure.

Instead, his mouth quirks up, and he releases a small huff of laughter. "I know you, Bianca. And when you lie, the right side of your mouth jerks slightly."

Does it? I reach up and touch my fingers to my lips. His grin widens.

My heart lurches, but not in fright. When he smiles like that, even though it is only momentary, my body responds to his nearness the way it always has. With a flash of need as inappropriate as it is unwanted.

I turn and stare out the window, trying to recreate distance between us. I raise my brows when I realize where we are. The limousine slows as it pulls up to the gates of Rio's Boston estate.

"Oh! I didn't think you'd ever come back here, after Francine…"

I swallow down the rest of my sentence. Francine was complicit in holding me captive, but she did it because Rio wanted her to, and she loved her nephew—her whole family —with all her heart. How can I blame her for that? I even grew to like her, in the end. She didn't deserve to die. Tears threaten, and I blink them away.

"I'm sorry about your aunt, Rio. I'm not sure I ever really told you, but she and I... I liked her. And I am sorry for your loss."

He grunts. "I haven't been back until now. And thank you. Francine was loyal to our family to her last breath."

There is a pause, and then he adds, "My aunt's memory will live on in all of us."

His last words puff against the back of my neck. I jerk and turn to face him. So close. His arm stretches behind my head along the back of the seat. If I tilt my head back, even a couple of inches, I could rest against his shoulder or upper arm.

The temptation to do so is almost overwhelming, especially when his fresh scent wafts up around me. The aftershave I always loved, subtle and sexy, teases at my nostrils and infuses my limbs with a sudden lethargy.

I look up into his face and read what he obviously wants me to see in this moment. Desire. Raw, naked desire, overlaid with a simmering anger.

I can't help myself. I reach up and cup his strong jawline. "Do you hate me, Rio, for what I did?"

He leans into my caress, for the merest second, before his eyes narrow and the moment of connection is gone. He shifts back slightly along the seat, and I drop my hand into my lap.

"I do not hate you. I hate what you did to me. And in my position, I cannot let that act go unpunished. You know that, do you not? Surely, you knew the consequences of defying me."

I clench and unclench my fingers, watching them almost dispassionately. "Yes, I knew. But I had to risk it. For her. Or him."

I rest my hand briefly over my stomach, and his gaze drops to study my bump.

"How are you going to punish me?" I wish my voice wasn't so husky. It betrays so much about the effect he has on me.

He is so big, so vital, that his very presence makes it hard to draw in a breath, let alone speak.

He opens his mouth, pauses as if considering his words, and then nods at the window. "We are here."

His announcement is a convenient change of subject, and I huff out a frustrated sigh.

The limo slows and then stops in front of the grand portico entrance of the estate I spent so much time in before I ran. The estate where we were married, in the chapel on the grounds of this grand home.

Other than the obvious desire to not be here in Boston at all, my feelings about returning are conflicted. I keep wondering where Francine was when she was gunned down. I know some of Rio's men also lost their lives in the gun battle here at the estate.

I'm not hugely superstitious, but even so, the thought of so much death right here in our home is unsettling. I'm sure there will be no trace of what happened, even though Rio by his own admission hasn't been back since then.

The place will have been cleaned and restored to its former glory, and life here has no doubt gone on as it always has, just like everything in this violent world into which I've been drawn.

A kick deep inside causes me to start, and I gently rub my belly, drawing strength from the knowledge my baby is well and making him or herself known. The limo driver has alighted and opens the door for us, but I pause when I realize Rio is staring at me intently.

Or to be more precise, he is staring again at my pregnant stomach, as if he too felt that kick.

Impossible, and yet he knew. The baby kicks again, and I jump.

He reaches out a hand, then stops with his fingers outstretched midair. "May I..."

*It's his child.* The thought ricochets through me like a pinball in an old-fashioned machine.

I ran from him to protect my baby from this life, from this world. But for the first time, it really hits me what I did to him.

I did the unforgivable. I took his child away.

---

## 6

*"If we are bold, love strikes away the chains of fear from our souls."*

Maya Angelou

*Bianca*

Rɪᴏ ʜᴀѕ ᴀѕ much right to be involved in this baby's life as I do. No matter who or what he is, saint, man, or monster.

"Of course," I answer, reaching forward to take his hand in mine.

I guide him to where I felt the last kick. He places his hand over my swollen abdomen, the gesture surprisingly intimate, and there is silence in the vehicle as we wait. His head is bowed. He's concentrating hard.

Just as I'm about to give up and suggest he move his hand away, another kick jabs at my insides. Rio lets out a strangled gasp. His eyes widen and his lips part slightly as he lifts his gaze to mine.

Tears fog my vision at the wonder in his expression.

I almost took this moment away from him.

I've been selfish, and even though I still think I did the right thing in trying to protect my baby from the world of organized crime, I cannot protect him or her from Rio. He has the right to know his own child. And every child has the right to know his or her father.

I do *not* have the right to remove their choice about being in each other's lives.

"I'm sorry, Rio." I squeeze his fingers, and despite my efforts to blink them back, a couple of tears escape. They drift silently down my cheeks, one dropping onto the back of our joined hands.

He uses his free hand to swipe at the wetness with the pad of his thumb. A shiver runs right through my body and centers in my core.

*Oh.* I didn't realize I could feel aroused while pregnant. I don't know if that's normal. I've never known anyone pregnant before Nita, and we hadn't gotten to the stage of speaking about intimate things like...*that.* The sensation between my thighs is a familiar ache, but somehow magnified a hundredfold from what it was when I was last with Rio in a sexual way.

Is that because I've missed him as much as I've feared him? I haven't felt turned on since the day I jumped on the bus to Augusta, but I craved his powerful presence in my life every single waking moment, even when I knew it was unhealthy.

He's my obsession. He was right when he talked in the past about love and hate being two sides of the same coin.

He must notice my reaction. It would be impossible not to when my thighs part almost involuntarily as if inviting his touch at the apex between them. My cheeks heat at the raw need that darkens his irises almost to black.

His hand on my belly tightens, and I brace, expecting him to lean in and claim my mouth with his.

*I am yours, Rio. Even if I don't want to be.* We both know it.

My lips part, and I wait. But in the end, he doesn't move toward me.

Instead, he says softly, "He's strong. That is a good thing."

There is pride in his tone.

Somehow, I manage a slight chuckle. "You mean *she* is strong. Of course she is. She has my blood. And yours."

He grunts. "We shall see. Boy or girl, Bianca, I will be content as long as our child is healthy."

The perfect answer. *Oh my God.* It's easier if he continues being a monster. This version of Rio doesn't seem monstrous at all, and that makes it so much harder to keep any barrier in place between us.

*Remember what he said*, I remind myself.

*I will not kill you. Yet. I will consider your future after the baby is born.*

Someone outside the car clears their throat, and the moment dissipates into thin air. I alight awkwardly from the vehicle, and two dark-suited goons step forward to grab me by the upper arms. They flank me, thereby ensuring I cannot move a step in any direction without their cooperation.

"Wait, Rio! What—"

"You know where to take her, Mitch," he says to the man standing on my left. "You have your instructions."

Then he turns, strides up the stairs marking the entrance, and disappears inside the building, leaving me with these two armed and expressionless strangers. Strangers who represent everything I tried to run from. Strangers who lead me through the front entrance in Rio's wake.

When I reach the foyer, I automatically start toward the staircase, but the man named Mitch jerks me in another direction altogether.

They guide me down the long hallway, past Rio's first-floor office and other rooms on that level, toward a small elevator near the back of the building that I noticed last time I was here but never got to explore. There's only one level above us, so I'm not surprised when the elevator heads down rather than up. The doors open to a corridor, brightly lit with fluorescent tubing and with concrete walls and floor.

How far underground are we? I had no idea there was a whole rabbit warren of rooms and hallways deep beneath the estate. What was going on beneath my feet while I lived in relative innocence up above?

My heart is racing by the time we stop in front of an open metal door. The whole place gives off prison vibes. When I glance inside to a fully decked-out bedroom and sitting room suite with gold- and white-wallpapered walls and thick cream carpet, I start shaking my head.

"No. No, no, no…" He's locking me, literally, in a dungeon? I joked in my mind about a dungeon and handcuffs, but I didn't actually expect… "Over my dead fucking body."

I plant my feet more firmly on the floor and brace my arms against the doorframe, but it's no use. One of the goons pries my clutching fingers off the frame, and the other picks me up and carries me over the threshold to my new home.

He plonks me down by the bed and moves quickly back to the door.

"Someone will deliver dinner in a couple of hours," the one named Mitch says, and then they're gone.

Just like that, I'm alone in this gilded cage. Imprisoned, yet again, by a Mafia monster and his team of goons.

---

*Rio*

I STAND at the window of my office at the estate and stare out at the setting sun. The French folding doors lead out from the office onto the neatly paved terrace and offer a view across the rolling gardens down toward the river that edges my property. The evening rays turn the vista golden orange, and if I were an emotional man, I might be moved by such a view.

Out of the corner of my eye, I catch a glimpse of the chapel where Bianca and I were married, and my mouth tightens at the memory of all that has happened since. That day seems a lifetime ago. Was it really less than a year?

Bianca has turned everything upside down since then.

I was looking for her for so long prior to that day, and I had no idea what I would do with her when I found her.

Just like now. What am I to do with my recalcitrant, runaway wife?

I may still be angry with her—and I was blazingly, incandescently angry in the beginning—about the fact that she ran, but I understand why she did it, and I cannot fault her for wanting to protect her child.

*Our* child.

This life is often violent, rarely safe, and all actions have consequences. Unfortunately for Bianca, my beautiful little bird, that includes her. No one can be an exception to that rule. If I allow one person to take advantage of me, my power base will topple and fall quicker than I can blink.

I do not *want* to punish my wife. I *have* to punish her. I have no choice.

I turn from the window to face my second, who must have the patience of a saint to put up with my recent moods day in and day out.

He has been standing silently waiting since he asked what we should do about Rossi. Waiting for me to be ready with an answer.

"Rossi is a problem that will need to be dealt with," I concede. "Sooner rather than later. But I still need him alive, for now. I am certain he has information about the past that he may not even know is valuable. I need that information, Danelli."

"Yes, Boss." My second's expression shows puzzlement. He rightfully expects more of an explanation.

I cannot tell him that I've been operating on gut instinct when it comes to Rossi, having suspected for some time that the deaths of my parents, and Bianca's, are linked, despite the crimes being several years apart. It would not be considered enough to have a gut feeling about something in my position. But now I have proof, and it is time to move.

"Carnarvon sent through a report this morning that confirms DNA found at my parents' murder scene matches a sample found at the scene of the bomb that killed Bianca's parents."

Danelli is good. He only reveals his shock via a slight widening of the eyes. "That link was only discovered now?"

"The testing was less advanced back then. I ordered a retest of all the evidence."

Danelli nods thoughtfully and doesn't need to ask how my men were able to gain access to forensic evidence from cold case files. He knows my methods that involve greasing the right hands, and using threats when bribery does not work.

"And Rossi is the common denominator?"

"He was an associate of my father's, and in love with Bianca's mother. He may not have been directly involved in their deaths, but I am certain he knows something. He is a conduit to the past—and I will keep him around until we no longer need him."

Danelli grunts. "Then he disappears?"

"Precisely."

I return to my desk and take a seat, leaning my elbows on the mahogany expanse and steepling my fingers as I study my second. "I spoke with Rossi again this afternoon. He, too, has heard more whispers of a new player on the scene who was apparently directing Anders and the men who followed him to oblivion in my club. He confirmed the name he had heard whispered as Antonio. Not Anton. Does that name ring a bell for you?"

"No, Boss. I mean, I do know a couple of Antonios—it's not an uncommon name," Danelli answers.

His face holds its usual furrowed brow. He is a good second, taking on the worries of our family almost as keenly as I do.

"But neither are what I'd consider players, and neither would have the balls to go up against you. They're small fish. One is an old guy who plays bocce at Langone Park, and the other owns a restaurant down near Battery Wharf."

"The wharf?" My attention sharpens. "I understand we've had some issues again down at the wharf, Danelli."

"I'm sure it's not related to this guy's restaurant, Boss. But I'll look into it. Same issue as the last two times?"

"Yes. Our shipments were held up, just long enough to raise a question mark over our ability to deliver on time. Check the shipment for tracking devices before it gets released to the client this time. And pay a visit to our friends on the payroll. I believe they need a reminder."

Danelli straightens. "Will do, Boss. How strong a message do we send?"

"The strongest." I know what that order means for at least one person, but there is no choice in the matter if I wish to avoid a far bigger bloodbath. One or perhaps two deaths to prevent many.

In the past, I would not have thought twice about delivering such an order. Now, I find myself wondering what Bianca would think if she were here in the room with us. Would she look at me with those sad, judgmental eyes and ask me to reconsider my decision? Would she find me wanting if I refuse?

"I will not tolerate betrayal, Danelli." *Except from my wife.* I shut down the inner taunt fast. "From *anyone.*"

He flinches at the sudden viciousness in my tone. "Yes, sir. I'm on it."

He turns to leave, then pauses.

"Yes?" I bark out.

"I'm wondering why Rossi's team was used in the attack on your club. And…" He swallows before adding, "Targeting your family here at the estate. Why commandeer someone else's team rather than set up their own? And why his in particular?"

It is a good question from my second, and one I have been pondering too. "I do not know the answer to that particular question. But as to why specifically Rossi's team was chosen, I believe that may have been in the hope of starting a war between two powerful families. Deflecting our attention from something else that may be about to happen."

Another reason to keep Rossi alive. For now. He is a piece of the puzzle; I am certain of it. I just don't know which part.

I wave a hand, dismissing Danelli. "Have the teams continue their search for information on the name Antonio. Get the Dartside PI team involved, too."

Is there a chance the recent attack by Anders could be linked to the past? No DNA matching my parents' crime scene was found at the club, or here at the estate, but that means nothing. Whoever ordered the hits on my family would be unlikely to have attended in person.

If the person who killed Bianca's parents was after the Carlotti inheritance, then he or she failed miserably. But why bring my parents into the mix and kill them several years later? What could they have to do with it? Back then, I was young and intent on partying. I was the heir, not the Boss. I had no knowledge of Bianca and certainly no plans to marry her or bring the Carlotti inheritance into the Agosti business.

My wife's family. My parents. My aunt. So much blood spilled already. And for what?

When I find the person or people responsible, there will be rivers of blood in retaliation. A war is brewing, and we have only seen the very beginning of the carnage.

## 7

_"Courage is grace under pressure."_
Ernest Hemingway

_Bianca_

MY FIRST INSTINCT when they shove me into this luxury prison and slam the door is to turn and bash my fists against the metal, shrieking until someone comes to let me out. Surely even Rio wouldn't be monstrous enough to leave me down here alone forever. Would he?

But even as I swivel toward the now-barred entrance, I stop short. I thought I was alone in the suite. But I'm not.

Two women are seated quietly on the settee in the living area of the suite. They are both watching me carefully. One has a stethoscope draped around her neck, and the other is dressed in nurse's scrubs.

Rio got me medical support? He locked me down here in

a dungeon, threatened to kill me, and yet he's arranged medical assistance? Nothing about Rio is ever easy or uncomplicated.

I fold my arms across my middle, feeling so many mixed emotions it's a miracle I don't spontaneously combust.

"I presume you're here to check me over and ensure my baby is healthy?"

The woman in scrubs gives me a small smile and points toward the king-sized bed between them and me, and I can't think of a reason not to comply. I cross the room and perch on the edge of the mattress. The one with the stethoscope looks less friendly. She starts forward while the other woman bends down to a bag on the low coffee table. She pulls out a blood pressure cuff and monitor and steps up with the obvious intention to attach it to my arm.

"I've just been kidnapped. Again. So, the reading might be a little high right now," I quip.

The doctor *tsk-tsks* me. "Don't be childish, Mrs. Agosti," she says, confirming my initial gut reaction. We will *not* be friends. "We're here to help you and ensure the remainder of your pregnancy is as stress free as possible."

Stress free? Stress fucking *free*?

She doesn't seem to notice my incredulous expression.

"I'm Doctor Conner," she continues smoothly, "and this is my assistant, Selina. Please cooperate, as that will be much better for the child. And for you."

She's right. I *hate* that she's right. And I know I'm being childish, but Rio has done the one thing that he knows I will hate more than anything. He has taken away my freedom. How long *will* he keep me down here? For the rest of my pregnancy?

Fear squeezes my heart. For the rest of my *life*? What if he never lets me out again?

Numbly, I hold out my arm and allow the nurse to attach the cuff and then adjust the monitor part of the machine. "So, are we all going to be dungeon buddies down here for the duration?"

Why can't I stop mouthing off? This isn't me. I hate that I'm acting like someone I don't recognize, someone with the insane urge to kick and scream and smash her fists against the wall in sheer frustration. Someone who spouts stupid snark every time she opens her mouth.

I clear my throat. "Look, I'm sorry." I try again. "I'm kind of rattled right now. This morning I was living in Cleveland, eating apple pie and ice cream with someone I thought was a friend. And now I'm... Yeah. Here. I'm sure you're both keen to help me and my baby, and I appreciate that."

For all my fear regarding Rio and what he may eventually do to me, that look in his eyes when he felt the baby kick told me he will never harm his own child. In Rio's world—in his mind—I may simply be an incubator for his child, but while that is the case, he is looking after both of us the best he can.

In his own twisted way.

The doctor smiles approvingly, as if she can hear the truth in my tone. We're finally on the same page.

"That's better," she says. "Now, if you don't mind, I'd like to give you a physical examination, and then we can have a chat and take some of your history, Mrs. Agosti."

"Sure." I lie back on the bed when they tell me to, and allow the doctor to poke and prod at my body and ask lots of questions.

Eventually, she pronounces herself satisfied with the state of my pregnancy.

"Though you could probably stand to eat a little more," she says, studying me from head to toe with a small frown. "I will leave word in relation to that when we head upstairs."

"Oh. So, you're *not* staying?"

Panic flutters in my chest. I'm absurdly upset by the notion of being left down here alone. I don't even know these two medical personnel, and yet I'm fearful at the thought of them leaving me.

The nurse, Selina, answers my query while the doctor packs up her bag. "It'll be fine, Mrs. Agosti. We'll be on call twenty-four seven and can be here in less than ten minutes."

"Please, call me Bianca," I automatically correct.

Mrs. Agosti is still too foreign. Bree Walker is long gone, and poor Aria Lowe from Cleveland barely had a chance to live. I stifle the urge to laugh, unwilling to explain what I find amusing, when the truth is actually the opposite.

Nothing about my life with Rio Agosti is amusing.

The nurse smiles at me again, oblivious to the angst raging in my head. "Bianca," she repeats. "We'll be in every couple of days for regular checkups, so you won't go through this alone. We'll bring a portable scanner next time, and the doctor will do some imaging."

That level of support is far more than I had in Cleveland. It is more than many people have even if they're not being held against their will.

"Thank you," I manage, knowing that a deep-down part of me is also thanking Rio.

I should be filled with rage, or terror, or both, for what he's done. And maybe I am, a bit. My feelings for Rio are so convoluted even I don't really understand them.

But the truth is, he *didn't* kill me for running, when he possibly would have if it had been anyone else.

And in sending down this clearly competent doctor and nurse to look after me, he is sending the message that he does place value on our child's well-being.

We do have that in common.

This time, the laugh does escape my throat before I can strangle the sound. A tiny chuckle, born of impending hysteria, but the moment is enough to lift the lips of both doctor and nurse in response to what they see as a positive reaction to the nurse's announcement.

If only they knew.

The nurse crosses the room and presses an intercom buzzer embedded in the wall beside the metal door, then slips out when it's opened, followed quickly by the doctor.

I catch a glimpse of Mitch and another goon stationed in the corridor before the door clangs shut behind them. I remember how Francine left the door unlocked once, when I first arrived at the suite above Rio's club, and how I ran, only to bounce straight off Rio's hard, muscled chest in the fire stairwell.

This time, I don't bother checking the door. Even if they did make the mistake of leaving it unlocked, there's no way I'd get past those goons, let alone make my way unseen out of this maze of underground rooms and off the estate.

And where would I go? Unlike last time, I have no money and no fake ID. Nowhere to run.

All the emotion I've been holding inside since I walked into my apartment building in Cleveland and saw those rings on the bathroom counter suddenly comes bubbling up from where I've held it deep inside. The only advantage of being trapped down here alone is that no one is around to witness my increasingly hysterical ugly crying.

*Rio*

I DON'T SEE Bianca for the next several days, not simply because I am a busy man, but because she creates unfamiliar emotions in me that I don't know how to deal with.

From the moment I was born, I was raised to be the head of this family. My father was a hard man, difficult to please, as he had to be to run the organization as successfully as he did. He instilled the same cold and dispassionate ruthlessness in me.

And he was proud of me for that.

He took me with him once to a "negotiation" the day after my thirteenth birthday. Said I was now a man and needed to understand fully what that meant. There was no negotiation that day. He killed every one of his enemies in the room, except one.

Then he handed me his gun and said, "Finish the job, Gregorio. Be a man."

I did, and he looked at me with approval for the first time in his life.

I never told him that I threw up when we got home, after I managed to get to my room. I never told him that I didn't sleep for many nights after that, reliving over and over the moment when the victim stared at me with terror in his eyes and pleaded for me to let him live. The smell of death. The look of it. The sheer messiness of it.

I couldn't get any of it out of my mind.

My mother knew of my struggles, and she told me to lock away the darkness in a box deep inside my heart, and to never let it out.

But the darkness is still there, buried so deep it has become part of the fabric of my being. It is always there, threatening to rise up and take over everything in a black haze of rage.

My father taught me that to be soft, is to risk death.

Bianca *softens* me. And as the head of the Agosti cartel, I cannot afford soft. I will *not* allow it.

And so, she remains in the bunker suite under lock and key, just as the darkness that coats my soul remains locked deep inside my heart.

## 8

---

*"...the amount of love you feel for someone and the impact
they have on you as a person, is in no way relative to the
amount of time you have known them."*
Ranata Suzuki

*Rio*

I WANT TO KEEP AWAY, but thoughts of Bianca fill my every
waking moment. Finally, I give in to the urge to check on her.
I head for the elevator and see the housekeeper waiting there
with a dinner tray, the button already lit.

When I take the tray and dismiss her, she shoots me a
shocked look, as if seeing me undertake such a menial task
hurts her sensibilities. The woman is not as efficient as
Francine was at running my household, but she is a fast
learner and I am certain, now we are in residence at the estate

once again, that things will soon run as smoothly as they did in the past.

"It is fine," I say. "I am heading down anyway. I must speak with my wife."

"Yes, sir." She scurries away, leaving me to deliver the food Bianca's obstetrician insists she needs—steak, vegetables, and orange juice to help with the absorption of iron.

"She seems well overall," Doctor Conner said before she left on that first day. "But I don't think she's been eating as well as she could. Make sure she gets fresh fruit and vegetables daily, and I would suggest red meat at least a couple of times a week to ensure she's receiving the iron she and the baby need. Walks in the garden, too, so she can get some sunlight, gentle exercise and fresh air. Not in the heat of the day, of course, but perhaps mornings or evenings. I will return in two days' time to check her again... unless you need us sooner?"

"If I do, you will be notified," I told her. I am paying her a fortune to be on call twenty-four seven, along with her nurse. If Bianca needs them, they have been contracted to be here within ten minutes. I chose her because she was on a list of the best three obstetricians in the city. The other two were men, and I will not tolerate another man getting anywhere near my wife's vagina, even in a professional, medical capacity.

When I enter Bianca's suite, she is curled up on the white settee in front of the electric fireplace. She's wearing a loose gray T-shirt that falls to her mid-thighs, her legs bare. Her feet are tucked up beneath her with only her toes peeping out, and I make a mental note to arrange a beautician for her nails now that she's back.

Not that she needs anything to make her more beautiful.

She has always had a natural beauty, even before I brought her here. Though right now, her face is blotchy, and it's clear she's been crying.

"I know it's summer up there in the real world," she says, "but down here, it's the same temperature day or night. It could be any day of the year, and I felt like staring into the flames."

I place her dinner on the low coffee table in front of her and take a seat in the armchair opposite. "You don't need my permission to light the fire, Bianca. This suite is yours."

"This dungeon, you mean."

A thrum of anger coats her voice. It makes my inner monster purr. She should be careful, lest she push too many of my buttons. I cannot guarantee what will happen if she pushes me too far.

"Call it whatever you wish. This is the price you pay for running from me."

"The price? The *price*?" She launches to her feet, and I wonder if she's about to run at me, but instead, she begins to pace. Her bare feet sink into the thick carpet, and her toes scrunch as if even they hold hidden rage. "I'm your *wife*, Rio, not your mortal enemy. You can't keep me locked down here forever. *Can you*?"

The last question comes out sounding like a wail. She stops pacing and wraps her arms across her middle as if trying to contain her angst. I've noticed she does that often, when she's upset.

The action pushes up her breasts, which are more rounded and fuller-looking than I remember them. The pregnancy, presumably, but the result is enticing, and I steeple my fingers in front of my lips, trying not to show a reaction.

"You have created a conundrum for me, dear wife." I'm

not sure she will accept my explanation, but it's the only one I have.

I almost laugh at my own vulnerability. I do not explain myself to others. Usually.

"As the boss of a large and powerful organization, my enemies are many, and most are waiting in the shadows to pounce the moment I show any weakness. You ran from me, Bianca, with my child in your womb, and if I do not take any action because of that, then not only will my enemies perceive me as weak, but they will recognize that you mean something more to me than perhaps they realized. They will use *you* as an opportunity to move against me."

Her brows knit as she considers my explanation. "So, does everyone know you're keeping me imprisoned down here?"

"Everyone who needs to know."

She pinches her bottom lip between thumb and forefinger. My cock twitches into life at the sensual action.

"It is a complex situation," I add. "You should not have run."

She huffs out a breath and drops her hand away from her mouth. "You're punishing me in a way that everyone can presumably respect, but in doing so, you're also keeping me safe? Because…you care about me?"

How can she doubt that? I treat her differently—with far more leeway—than I would any other human being. "I have not hidden the effect you have on me, Bianca. But one might deduce, from the fact that *you* contacted the Feds and then ran, that *you* do not care about *me*."

"I… Well…"

"Hmmm?"

"You know that's not true, Rio. I left you that note. To explain…"

"Ah, yes. The note. You said you loved me. That's right."

"I did say that. Because it's true." She gently rubs her baby bump.

I'm not sure if the action is deliberate, to curry my favor, or unconscious. From her slightly unfocused expression as she shifts her gaze back to the flames in the fireplace, I suspect the latter.

"I always will love you," she says, after a minute of silence. "Even though I ran. Even though I'm mad as hell that you've brought me back and locked me up down here. My feelings for you—*about* you—are very…complicated, Rio."

"Yes. As are mine for you."

Everything about Bianca unsettles me. I clamp down on my swirling thoughts, breathe slowly and steadily to calm my system, and point to her food.

"You need to eat before your dinner grows cold."

"I'm not hungry."

"Bianca. Your stomach has growled twice since I entered the room." I stare at her, and she throws her hands up in the air.

"Fine."

She stomps back to the couch and sits once again, staring at the tray in front of her before finally taking up the utensils and eating. There is silence in the room while she does so, the hiss of the fake fire making a surprisingly restful background noise. I lean back in my chair and concentrate for a while on the dance of golden orange flames in the grate, understanding why she wanted the fire on even though the temperature down here is kept at an even keel.

Eventually, she pushes back the tray and lets out a puff of laughter. "The chef knows his or her stuff. Is it the same one as…before?"

She leans back on the couch and tucks her feet up under her once again. She looks so young and innocent, but her eyes hold a sadness that wasn't there a few minutes ago. She liked Francine, I remember, and she spent a lot more time in my aunt's company than I did over the past year.

"All the surviving staff returned once the estate was repaired and…cleaned." My hesitation is slight, but Bianca's gaze cuts straight to mine.

She knows me. And she knows how much my aunt's death eats at my conscience. Francine did not deserve to be gunned down simply because she was related to me.

Her blood—literally—was spilled on the steps of this home, and she will be avenged. I will make certain of it.

"The security detail has since been doubled," I add, wanting to reassure her of her safety. "And additional measures have been put in place around the estate. These underground rooms are as secure as it gets. I am in the process of moving my office down here, too. No one will get through to you in this bunker, Bianca. I can assure you. They won't get past me or my men twice."

"I believe you." She still looks fragile, but there is a hint of color in her cheeks since eating that gives her a healthier glow.

Satisfaction courses through me. I circle back to answer one of her earlier questions.

"If you behave, you will not need to remain down here forever. I simply need to make a statement by keeping you locked up for a period of time."

"Oh? Well, at least that's something." Her eyes glitter, and this time not with sadness. Fresh anger threads through her tone once again. "You may take the tray away now, Rio. I'm going to have a shower."

She unfolds her legs and stands, and my hunter instincts rise. I stand, too, not willing to allow her to get away with that imperious taunt.

"You already had a shower," I caution. "I could smell the fresh scent of soap and shampoo wafting off your hair and skin the moment I entered the suite."

"I... Well." She tosses back her hair. "I need another."

She turns in the direction of the bathroom, but gives away her uncertainty about my reaction when she flicks a glance over her shoulder. I take a couple of steps toward her, and her eyes widen when she notices my arousal. My cock is hard and ready; it has been since the moment she pulled at her delicious, plump bottom lip.

The whole place smells of her and reminds me of all the times in the past we lay tangled in each other's arms.

Her mouth—her beautiful, generous mouth—parts slightly, and she turns and scurries into the bathroom. The door slams shut.

*Oh, little bird. You will not get away from me that easily.*

I stalk across the space and thrust the door open just as fiercely as she closed it. It swings wide, and the force of the momentum smashes the handle against the wall. She whirls to face me from where she's standing clutching the edge of the sink.

"Rio, please get out. I don't want this."

"You don't?"

I cover the few feet between us. She can't retreat. Her ass

is pressed against the edge of the countertop, my erection pushing against her belly.

I pin her between my arms, covering her hands still gripping the counter edge with my own. No escape. "Are you certain you don't want this, Bianca? It has been a while."

"I…" Her eyes dart to my lips, and the tip of her tongue dips out to moisten her own.

I grin down at her, but I doubt my expression conveys a friendly vibe. "Tell me truthfully you haven't craved my touch the way I crave yours, and I will walk out of here and leave you alone."

A tiny whimper escapes her, and she shakes her head.

"We both know you can't tell me that. And if you try, it will be a lie."

"I don't… I… Rio, please…"

"Please what, Bianca? Truth. *Now*."

"I want…"

I lean forward so I can whisper in her ear. "What do you want, Bianca? Tell me, and I may decide to give it to you. Right here, right now. You want me to leave you alone? Or you want me in that shower, or atop this counter? Or do you prefer me to lift you up and carry you out there to your soft, comfortable bed, where I will bury my head between those delectable thighs of yours and dip into your delicious, fertile core with my eager tongue?"

She groans. "I don't know if we can. Is it safe? I want… Oh God, Rio. I *want*…so badly. I can't, ever, seem to find the strength to say no to you."

She doesn't know if we can? Illumination hits, and I release one of her hands to smooth a lock of loose dark hair back off her face.

"I confirmed with your doctor before she left today, Bianca. Because you are well, sex is safe right up until the birth, as long as you feel up to it. Do you feel up to it, my wife? Because I have craved you as much as I hated you, every waking moment, since you ran."

## 9

*"Hate the sin. Love the sinner."*
Mahatma Gandhi

*Bianca*

SEX IS *safe up until the birth.*

*Oh, thank God. Thank God.*

My body is on fire with need. I don't want to admit that to myself or to him, but I don't need to. Rio knows my desires as intimately as he knows my fears. My legs threaten to buckle as the ache in my breasts and at my core grows more insistent.

Does pregnancy make sexual need stronger? I don't remember this level of arousal before. This deep, powerful craving that seems to be taking over every part of my mind and crashes through my body in waves.

"I don't want to be here, Rio. I don't want to be stuck in

this basement prison of yours. But I still want *this*." I lift my free hand and splay it on his chest. "I want *you*."

God help me, I'm still sick for him.

I try to build self-disgust in my thoughts, hoping it will calm the inappropriate desire, but there's no point. My mind won't cooperate. My body has gone past the point of reason.

I want him. I *love* him. I need him. And he can probably do whatever he wants with me, barring hurting our child, and I will accept it.

"Of course you do, Bianca. You are *mine*. And we are meant to be together, whether either one of us likes that fact or not."

When he pushes strands of hair out of my eyes and caresses my cheek with a warm, insistent thumb, all I can think of is how that thumb will feel on my clit, drawing circles around the swollen bud until I buck beneath his touch and cry out in satiation.

I want him. I want *this*, and yes, I hate him for imprisoning me again. But he's my husband, and I love him.

I love-hate Rio Agosti, and I've *missed* him so damn much it hurts.

I lift my arms and wrap them around his neck. When he dips his head and takes my mouth—claims me once again as his—I feel rather than hear his satisfied groan, like a deep vibration that reverberates inside my own chest.

He tastes faintly of whiskey and cigars, as well as something uniquely Rio, a taste I haven't forgotten, but the reality of it is far more alluring than the memory. I moan as his tongue tangles with mine, exploring, possessing me...

And then he breaks off the kiss and hefts me up into his arms.

67

I gasp and smack him gently on the shoulder. "No, Rio. Wait. I'm too heavy…"

He ignores me, instead turning and heading back into the bedroom area of the suite and lowering me onto the comforter that decorates the bed. "Never too heavy for me, *la mia bellissima moglie*."

I shrug off my loose T-shirt and then lift my butt to assist him in sliding down my underwear. His fingertips graze my hips and thighs in the lightest of touches, and I shiver as goose bumps rise up.

"I'm pregnant, not breakable," I tease, lying back on the bed.

I allow my knees to drop so my pussy is exposed. He shucks off only his shoes and crawls onto the bed, still fully clothed. He kneels between my legs, forcing my legs farther apart, and then lowers his head.

When the tip of his tongue laps at my seam, I arch up and into him, wanting more. Needing more. Needing all of him. His fingers dance on my inner thighs, still too light for my liking, making swirls and patterns as he tongues my clit and then works his way down to my channel entrance.

I feel so full, so swollen and aching, that I don't know how long I'll be able to last. It's as if being pregnant has enhanced all the nerve endings in that area, and a moan escapes me at the exquisite sensations he's creating there as I clutch at the comforter with desperate fingers.

"So delicious," he murmurs. The words are a welcome hum against my flesh. "You are wet and swollen and ready, and we have hardly begun."

"*Rio.*" His name is a whimper on my lips.

I close my eyes, blocking out the view of the ceiling above us. I don't want to think about where we are right now, the circumstances that brought us back together. My need is too great, too urgent.

*Think later*, my brain whispers. Feel *now*.

And I do. Every stroke, every touch, every lick as he laps at my juices and brings me to the brink of an orgasm with his clever tongue and fingers.

Then he's gone, cool air between my legs replacing his hot breath and mouth. I open my eyes and lift my head, wanting him back. Wanting the mindless sensations that his presence ignites in my body.

He hasn't gone far. He is standing at the side of the bed, staring down at me. His eyes are dark and unreadable, his mouth shiny with my juices.

"Come back, Rio. Make love to me, please. I need you. *All* of you." I reach for his trousers, intending to unbutton and release his obviously erect organ.

But he takes a small step backward, just out of my reach.

"What...?"

"You are mine, Bianca. *Mine*. Never forget that."

I struggle up to sitting, not sure what he needs from me. "And I'm yours. I've always been yours, since the moment we met."

But still he doesn't come back to me. "When you ran, you tore my heart to shreds. No one has ever held that level of power or control over me, Bianca. *No one*."

His expression changes instantly from unreadable to pain-filled.

Pain-filled, and edged with fury.

"I wanted to kill you when you left. Did you know that, dear wife?"

Okay, this isn't going the way I expected. There's some-

69

thing riding him that wasn't there moments earlier. Something dark and inherently dangerous.

This is the "something" I ran from.

I bring my knees up toward my chest and wrap my arms around them. I move slowly, my heart rate catapulting into overdrive. I don't want to do anything to spook the beast.

"I guessed it would be like that," I whisper. "I'm sorry, Rio. Truly I am. I genuinely thought my decision was for the best."

I shrink down, trying to make myself smaller, hardly breathing at all. I want to seem less of a target for whatever darkness is driving him.

We remain like that for several seconds, unmoving, until he blinks a few times and shakes his head.

His shoulders drop slightly. "I have tried not to let you witness it, Bianca. There is a darkness in me…"

"I know." My heart is still pounding from the adrenaline rush born of terror, but the angst in his expression is real, and it hurts me to see it. "It's okay. I already know. And I still love you."

It's *not* okay. Not in any way. But right now, it seems important for him to hear otherwise.

"I need you, Bianca. I need…" His voice is hoarse, rough, and there's a sudden uncertainty in his expression that I've never seen before.

I could roll away, justifiably so given the terror that still races through my body. But if I do that—if I reject him in this moment—it may mean something more than either one of us can fully understand. And it may have deadly consequences.

I reach out a hand toward him, noting the trembling in my fingers. "Come here, Rio. Come to me. I need you, too. Please."

He steps forward, and allows me to unbutton and release his cock. He doesn't remove any other part of his clothing. Then he lunges forward, onto the bed, kneeling over me and pinning my hands above my head before I can suck in a breath.

His eyes are dark pools of emotion. So many emotions swirling in their depths. His mouth is set, and he's obviously fighting to remain in control. "I need to be inside you. You are *mine*."

His hands release mine to explore all over me, stroking my breasts, my stomach, my hips, and down to my mound in a frenzied manner. I can't keep up with his touch. It's like he needs to claim every inch of me as his, so I lie there and let him do what he needs.

Finally, he stills, and I am free to take his cock and guide it to my entrance. I am so wet and ready it would be embarrassing if it weren't for the growl that hisses out from his lips as the head of his organ dips easily into my core. "God, Bianca. I cannot hold on. Not now. Not like this."

"Don't hold on." I arch up, and he thrusts, seating himself fully inside me.

I gasp at the beautiful intrusion.

"Mine," he says again, over and over, punctuating each word with a pounding drive.

Deep. Deeper. Until I cannot deny it any longer.

Monster or man. Or both. It doesn't matter.

He *owns* me.

"Yours."

The connection stretches out with exquisite torture as he continues to buck and groan, and my need builds to impossible levels. I scream his name as I shatter, my core pulsing around him as he, too, reaches the edge and topples over into orgasm with a huge, growling roar.

My ecstasy immediately plummets and I struggle to hold back a sob at the remembrance of the raging darkness inside him, and the knowledge that the beast, whatever it is, is an integral part of him.

We can pretend, right now in this moment, that our marriage can be repaired and that we can live a life full of happiness and bliss, but that is all it would be. Pretend.

The reality is something quite different, and this bliss will soon be gone when the cold, harsh light of the outside world returns.

# 1 0

*"It is easier to forgive an enemy than to forgive a friend."*
William Blake

*Rio*

I HAVE ORGANIZED the meeting with Rossi here at the estate because this is my territory, and it will put him offside. I need him offside for this first face-to-face meeting since Danelli took the little finger of his left hand.

Bianca made no secret she was horrified at that news, but Rossi got off lightly, and he knows it.

Today, I want to look into his eyes and ensure he is telling the truth. And if he is not, it won't simply be another finger that he loses. It will be every appendage. If he is my enemy, then I want him to know fear before he dies for crossing me.

Danelli is situated near the door, and several of his Alpha

team are here in the library but stationed discreetly so I can converse with Rossi without everyone overhearing us.

I cringe a little when my second references his team in those terms. He loves anything military, and I indulge his need to name the various security details in that way. Suffice for me to know that Danelli's Alpha team includes his best men, and I am confident we have the security we need to maintain control should Rossi have any plans to double-cross me.

Unlikely, given my insistence that he leave his security at the gate, but after some posturing, he agreed to the stipulation because he knows he has no choice.

I have a little surprise in store for him later, but first, we must talk business.

When Rossi is escorted into the room we call the informal living area, I turn from the tall floor-to-ceiling windows that face out onto the expanse of grass that runs down to the river. From here, I cannot see the chapel, and for once, I am grateful. I need a clear head today, and I cannot afford to dwell on Bianca.

She muddies my thoughts and makes me question every decision. Especially the difficult, morally gray choices. Every time I'm with her, it is like she reaches deep inside me and tweaks something, fine-tuning me, and I leave the encounter irrevocably changed.

No one has ever had that effect on me before, and I don't like the feeling of uncertainty it brings.

Uncertainty, in my position, can mean the difference between life and death.

Clear blue sky and bright sunshine abound outside, but here in my domain, the temperature is kept cool, and the dark wood of my furniture and the stacks of books lining two of the walls cast endless shadows within the room.

I live in the shadows. It seems appropriate to meet another of my kind here.

I deliberately remain by the window, my back to the view, forcing him to head across the carpet toward me. Sunlight hits his face.

"Rio, my old friend. It is good to see you in person once again."

"Is it?" I ask with a smile. Rossi instantly stills, knowing a smile from me does not mean I am feeling joyous. "Old friend."

He hovers, as if unsure what to do, then he seems to gather himself and continues across before stopping in front of me.

I glance down at his clenched hands, minus any bandaging. "The wound has healed, then?"

"Mostly." He shrugs. "It hurts still, but the scarring is minimal, and there's no sign of infection."

There is a hint of deference in his manner that I have not seen in previous visits. He is clearly wary—rightfully so.

"I gave you back your wife, to show good faith," he says, reproach lacing his tone.

"You *gave* her back?" I arch my brows, showing him that I recognize and dismiss his blatant stretching of fact.

"W-well," he stutters, "I gave you the information you needed to start the search for her. I gave you the location and her new name."

I grunt, acknowledging there is a kernel of truth in his words. But he will not get off the hook that easily. "You gave me the information, *after* giving her the means to escape in the first place."

"I... Well...I..." His Adam's apple bobs. "She was already running, with help from the Feds. I simply thought I would step in and keep tabs on her. Ensure her whereabouts would not become a mystery. I always planned to keep you apprised."

"Did you?"

He rubs his palms together, then winces and drops them back to his sides. "I swear to you, on my *family*, Rio, that I did not know Anders was planning what he did. I have offered you my sincerest condolences regarding your aunt, and I have offered you the use of my men—my own resources—to find and destroy who did this to you. And remember, they did this to both of us, not just to you."

I study his face, lit up by the sunlight pouring into the room, and look for any sign of deception. He blinks, clearly uncomfortable with the brightness, but his eyes don't dart around or slide away. No muscle tic. No sheen of sweat. No change in his vocal tone. Nothing.

"I have said many times since that day, Rio, that I would have told you where she was. I'm certain you believe me, or I would no longer be breathing. Correct?"

The old man still knows how to play the game, it seems.

Slowly, I nod, and then gesture to the nearby couch. I will never again accept his hand, or call him friend other than in jest, but I have not yet pulled my gun and shot him between the eyes.

A good day for Rossi. So far.

He knows it, too.

The taut line of his shoulders relaxes just a notch when I say, "Take a seat and talk to me."

"Thank you, my friend."

I ignore the friend comment. *Keep your enemies close.*

I sit opposite where Rossi has settled. "You know how my family was impacted that day. And you and I both know that, by using your man to do it, whoever ordered the hit on me and my family likely wanted to start a war between us."

"Indeed." His dark eyes sharpen.

I am reminded that it would not do for anyone—me included—to underestimate this man.

At a signal from me, one of Danelli's men rushes forward with a cigar case. I gesture, confirming he may offer it first to the older man.

Once our cigars are cut and lit, I lean back on the couch. "Who would benefit from a war between us, Rossi? That is the question I need answered."

He leans forward, resting his hands on his knees. Smoke curls upward from the cigar held loosely between the fingers of his right hand.

"I do not know for sure, but I am willing to bet it has something to do with this…Antonio," he says, almost spitting out the name. "And I am only telling you this next fact because I hear whispers you are having similar issues to us down at the wharf, but we had a truck leave our warehouse outside New York and never arrive at its destination."

I only just manage to control my shock and take a moment to steady my breathing. "Destined for where?"

"Destined for our warehouse in Albany."

"Let me get this straight. One of your trucks—a whole shipment—has literally disappeared?"

"It has." Rossi leans back, his expression grim, before looking down at his cigar as if only just remembering it. He sucks on it furiously.

My pulse rate speeds up, but I do my best not to show my unease.

Unlike Rossi, I lift the cigar and take a pull in a slow and measured manner, before saying, "Then the war has already begun, Carlos, and we still do not know who our enemy is. I anticipated this, and I have already called a board meeting."

Rossi's eyes widen, and his mouth parts slightly. "The family heads? All of them? Together again in one room? When? And more importantly, where?"

I grin at him, aware that the grin does not reach my eyes. "This evening. Here at the estate. How convenient that you are already here. And yes, it has been three years since we were all under the same roof together. But it is time. We must unite against our common enemy, and then we have to bring him down before we are undone ourselves. Old *friend*."

---

*Bianca*

THE WOMAN who brings my lunch gives me a heads-up that I may be called upon to attend a meeting later today, and I should dress accordingly. What does that mean? What sort of meeting, and who will be there?

She simply shrugs when I ask and leaves me alone to eat yet another solitary meal.

It has been a week since I last saw Rio. Since he dropped his guard and revealed more of himself than I knew how to deal with. Since his monster reared up and scared me half to death.

I assume that's why he's steered clear since then. Because I can't imagine he enjoyed exposing any part of his inner self, even to me.

I don't want to love him, but I do. And I'm guessing he

feels the same complex push-pull, love-hate thing when it comes to me.

I've tried to do as he said since that night, and be as cooperative as I can. The doctor and nurse have been in every second day to check on me, and two of the goons take me upstairs and let me walk in the gardens twice a day—morning and early evening.

I always strain for a glimpse of Rio, but he must sequester himself away at those times because I've not caught even the faintest hint of his presence since he left my bed that night.

I only know he's still in residence here because I asked the nurse, Selina.

The summons to attend one of his meetings comes as a surprise. I assume he wants me there so he can send some kind of message to his business cronies. Probably to show them that I'm firmly back under his control.

He's made no secret of the fact that he still desires me, but he's also been candid about the damage I caused to the family by running away.

*I need to make a statement by locking you up*, he said when he brought me here.

That "statement" began the moment he placed me down here and removed my freedom. Again. He knows how much I hated that last time. And when he commands that I attend a meeting of his choosing, without giving me any information at all about where, why, or with whom, he compounds the punishment by confirming—to me and to everyone who matters—that I have no autonomy. No choice about anything except the requirement to serve his needs.

I debate the wisdom of pulling on a set of comfortable PJs and climbing into bed for an afternoon nap, but no doubt that will simply delay the inevitable. So, in the end, I shower and dress in what I think may be suitable attire for a business meeting, and then I sit and wait.

After half an hour, I begin to second-guess myself. Now I'm thinking he probably doesn't want me to look "businesslike" at all. I know Rio, and I know this male-dominated lifestyle. Women, whether wives or mistresses, are for display only. They are window dressing, and what he most likely expects from me at this meeting is a show of support from a woman who repents her bad behavior and will do anything to get back into his good graces.

I could try to defy him, but it would be a fight I'd surely lose. What can I do, stuck down here? My mind circles back again to my decision to cooperate. The best thing for me, and my baby, is to comply with his wishes as much as I can, and eventually, he may trust me enough to give me back my freedom.

I'm not sure if that's the full truth, but my mind shies away from facing any other reason. The way he looked at me when he last left, with warmth softening the hard planes of his face. The surprised delight in his expression—quickly brought under control, but I saw it—when our baby kicked for the first time beneath his touch.

*No, don't think about that. Don't humanize him. He's still a monster. He took Rossi's finger off, for Christ's sake.*

I slide out of the charcoal maternity trousers and white satin shirt that I had chosen because the clever cut of it hid my baby bump, and flick through various other clothing items in my walk-in wardrobe. Finally, I settle on a burgundy minidress that is so figure-hugging it will leave nothing to the imagination.

Deep down, I suspect Rio will want to remind whoever is

at the meeting that the woman who gave him the Carlotti outfit is now expecting his child.

And if he wants to show off his pregnant wife? This is the outfit to achieve that.

I am dressed and fully made up in what I call my classy mob-wife look when they come for me.

Two goons, as though I might somehow be able to evade the escort and run if he sends only one.

Neither of these men is familiar, and I remember with a pang that my favorite goon, Leon, was gunned down that day in the club. Gunned down while trying to protect me.

I try to put that out of my mind and let them lead me out of my dungeon suite and along a concrete corridor. My spiked heels click-clack as we walk. When we reach the elevator at the end of the corridor and step into the car, both men remain silent.

We ride up a level, and I expect to emerge into the soft evening warmth of Rio's estate home, but when the doors open, it seems we are still underground.

Another level between the house and my dungeon? Does Rio have a whole city carved out beneath the house I once lived in? How many levels are down here?

The goons still don't speak, but one stops before a solid-looking door before knocking and then gesturing me inside when someone opens it. My heart is already racing, and now I have trouble swallowing as all the saliva in my mouth and throat seems to dry up.

What will I find on the inside? What does Rio really want with me? It was safe for me to toy with the idea that he wants to show me off, but what if I'm completely wrong? Am I about to slide into danger once again?

## 11

*"Where there is unity there is always victory."*
Pubilius Syrus

*Bianca*

I LACE my fingers together in front of my baby bump, feeling extra protective all of a sudden, before I step into what appears to be a long and luxuriously decked-out conference room.

And then I stop short.

A dozen sets of eyes—more if you count the security dotted around the space—gaze at me with varying degrees of either indifference or curiosity. All older men, all expensively dressed in suits, and all seated around a huge rectangular conference table. Rio sits at the head of the table, watching my entrance with an implacable expression.

He rises when I enter. After a moment, the other men

glance at him and then rise too. I am certain their action of respect is for Rio's benefit, not mine.

Are these the heads of family, or their representatives, that I have heard about but never met collectively like this?

"Come in, dear wife," Rio says, his dark gaze still giving nothing away. "Join us at the table. Gentlemen, you all remember Bianca Carlotti-Agosti from our wedding, do you not? As you can see, she is back with me now, and expecting my child."

I was right, then.

*I'm glad I dressed up* is all I can think as I make my way around the table to where Rio still stands with one hand outstretched. I clasp his proffered hand, grateful for the familiar warmth in this sea of strangers. Even if that momentary comfort is offered by Rio himself.

Wait. Not all are strangers. One set of eyes is warmer than the others, and I realize with a flare of mixed emotions that Carlos Rossi sits at this table too.

I can't help my gaze dropping to his hands, searching for the damage inflicted by Rio. I'm not exactly sure what I should be feeling about this man. He was supposed to help me escape this life, and instead, he gave up information to my husband to save his own ass. But to be fair, I tricked him, too, and used his money to run farther than he had planned for me.

And now he has to deal with one less finger on one of his hands.

Rio draws me into his side and murmurs in my ear, so quietly that I'm certain no one else picks up the words. "A united front, little bird. That is what I need."

I shoot a glance upward and wonder if I'm the only one who can see how much tension he's holding. That tight jawline and the way his shoulders hunch up slightly, too high for comfort, give it away.

He must be dealing with a devil of a stress headache.

The stakes here are obviously high, and dread curls in my stomach as the truth becomes apparent. In this world, and in the helpless circumstances in which I currently find myself, Rio is truly the only one I can trust to keep my baby safe from any circling sharks.

These men are the sharks. And their sharp eyes are searching for any hint of weakness.

I bite the inside of my cheek to stop a completely inappropriate laugh from bursting free. It would be a laugh born of irony, not humor, but I'm sure no one at this table would take it that way. As if running from the man I love is not ludicrous enough, now I face the reality that the man I both love and fear is the only person I know who may offer a safe haven for me and my child.

I press into him, giving him a tiny nod, relaxing slightly at the flash of approval in his dark eyes. "Good girl."

He holds out a chair, and I take a seat between him and Rossi, who sits closest. I turn to the latter and shoot him a small, polite smile, even though I feel anything but friendly toward him.

I lean in and say quietly to the older man, "I'm sorry about your hand."

He immediately removes both of his hands from the table and tucks them in his lap.

The subject is clearly off-limits, so I change tack slightly. "I always planned to work out a way to pay you back the money you gave me. I do promise you that."

"Oh, I believe you, my dear," he whispers back, equally quietly. "But the fact is, you betrayed me, and so I chose to betray you. I am a pragmatic person, after all, and I know what I need to do to keep your husband onside."

"Betrayal in every direction, it seems," I answer, and this time I don't bother to keep my voice low.

A chuckle, quickly muffled, comes from someone else in the room, and Rio lays a hand on my thigh and squeezes. A warning to behave? I set my hands on the table in front of me, clasping them tight and hoping no one can see how much my fingers are trembling.

*I am Rio's wife*, I remind myself. And as such, they are unlikely to harm me in his presence.

I swallow down my fear, lift my eyes, and slowly work my way around the table, meeting the gaze of every man here. One after the other. I study their features, catalogue their gazes, and mark which ones hold disdain, disinterest, or actual hatred.

I may be the youngest person in the room. I may be the only female in the room. But I will not let a bunch of old-man thugs intimidate me.

*Yeah, right.* My mind taunts me. *And you're so brave you're ready to duck under the table if one of them looks at you sideways.*

After several seconds of silence, one of the men about halfway down the table inclines his head in a respectful manner. "She has courage, Agosti. I'll give her that. You chose well."

"I did, Enzo," Rio confirms, and the hand on my thigh squeezes again, but this time gently.

Then his fingers wander up, grazing briefly across my mound and causing a ripple of awareness to shiver over my skin. There's a tiny huff of breath from my husband, a sound that confirms he has noted my response to his touch and would do so much more if we were alone.

Then he turns his attention back to the room and leans forward, shifting from that hint of sensual to all-business in the blink of an eye.

"You are likely wondering why I have brought you all together at this time. The heads of family—all except Gianni Martelli, who is currently en route from Italy back to the States. Some of you I haven't seen for almost three years."

Murmuring breaks out around the table, and a few of those seated shift uncomfortably, as if they are unsure what my husband is about to say. Did they come here today, wondering if they would be gunned down? There is security in the room, but as I glance around, I note that all of the men seem to be Rio's own. These heads of family, if that's who they are, must be as uncomfortable as me in this situation, without their security accompanying them.

Far more so than me, probably. At least I have Rio and his team on my side.

As much as Rio *is* the monster everyone says he is, I am beginning to understand that, when I'm involved, he is less monstrous than people expect. I don't believe he would deliberately bring me into this room if he were expecting—or indeed, planning—some kind of massacre.

He confirms this when he spears each of the meeting attendees with a hard look and speaks in a loud, clear tone. "I have brought you all here to Boston for a frank discussion. It appears we have a common enemy, gentlemen. Someone who has begun to make moves on the chessboard. Trying to pit us against one another. Small disruptions at the wharf, or deliveries that never arrive. Have any of you... Ah, Enzo. I can see from your start of shock that you too have experienced similar."

The man addressed by Rio nods, a short, sharp movement that indicates he did not wish to share that information with this room.

"One of our warehouses down south burned down three weeks ago, the goods inside completely destroyed," he confirms.

A balding man with a goatee beard seated at the other end of the table to Rio and me grunts. "Interesting. One of our facilities was raided a month ago by the Feds. They had a tip-off, apparently, and it took a lot of maneuvering by our legal team, and discreet payoffs, to extricate several of our employees from the mess they found themselves in."

Rio lifts his chin and stares down the table at the goateed man. "Have you identified the source of the leak, Darov?"

I can't help shrinking down slightly in my seat. I remember when I was a child at school and the teacher asked who had drawn the rude picture on her whiteboard. Of course, it wasn't me, but my face still heated in a blush as the teacher's gaze roamed the room.

Everyone here probably knows I was approached by the Feds. Do they think it was me who gave them the tip-off for this man, Darov?

I would have never been able to give Rio up. I love him too much. But it has been made clear to me that my call to Felicity did start a chain of events that caused him some grief, and his lawyer, Carnarvon, had to work hard to keep him and several of his men out of the law's clutches.

"I have not identified the leak," the man concedes. "There was talk that it was someone from the Martelli outfit." He glares around the room. "And it is interesting that his is the only family not represented here today." Then he grunts. "But when my men looked into it further, they found nothing. If, as you say, there is someone working to pit us against each other, then it is only a matter of time before the situation escalates."

Rio nods. "Precisely. The chaos, death, and destruction that would follow will provide a perfect cover for someone to stroll in and take over while we are all at each other's throats."

The tension in the room ramps up as everyone stares suspiciously at each other. I automatically lean in closer to Rio. I don't know most of these men, but if they are the heads of Mafia outfits from around the Northeast region, then this gathering of people is quite possibly one of the most dangerous in the country right now.

"That is why we are here," Rio says. "To ensure that the balance of power does not shift. To reopen lines of communication between us that have lapsed over time. If we unite against our common enemy, then he will not succeed. And when we identify who he is…"

*Or she*, I think mutinously. *It* could *be a woman*.

He stands and stares around at everyone, then slams a fist down on the table. I jump in shock, noticing that I'm not the only one who does so.

*"Then we will crush him into dust."*

Amidst the murmurs, this time of approval and agreement, I suddenly have trouble breathing. This is the side of my husband I fear. The side I glimpsed when we were last together. The violent side, in a world that offers a kill-or-be-killed viewpoint. All of these people seem to understand and accept that as the norm.

But it isn't the norm. It isn't okay to lop people's fingers off because they annoy you, or want to crush someone into literal dust.

As if Rio can sense my distress, he drags me to my feet and slides an arm around my waist.

*Unity. A show of strength.*

His touch is both possessive and comforting. Which is crazy when he also terrifies me.

Regardless of my churning emotions, he is sending a clear message to everyone here that I am his and therefore not to be touched. I raise my chin and slip my arm around him, too. He wants to show us united? Here we are, Mafia Dons.

As scared as I am about my future, I take some comfort from the knowledge that Rio will do all he can to protect me and the baby if a turf war does break out.

I press against him, taking a deep breath and letting it out in a slow exhale, trying to remain calm, at least outwardly.

I will not crumble. I am strong. I have to be strong for the baby.

Because in this violent world in which I once again find myself, the strong are the only ones who survive. And anyone weak will be annihilated.

Crushed into dust.

## 12

*"Our greatest glory is not in never failing, but in rising up
every time we fail."*
Ralph Waldo Emerson

*Bianca*

Rio and his business guests spend more time talking, but the
attention is no longer on me as they start to nut out varying
theories and plans of action. Whoever their enemy is, the
person most likely doesn't have long to live. These are some
of the most powerful men in the country, and if they can
unite and share their resources, there will be no stopping
them.

I think back with a pang of nostalgia to the days when I
worked at the Animal Paws center, where my hours were
filled with feeding, bathing, and walking dogs, and caring for
other sick and abandoned animals. I was surrounded then by

happy, carefree people who, like me, loved their job and enjoyed the idea of helping creatures in need.

A year ago, I would never in a million years have imagined myself sitting in a conference room with a bunch of Mafia bosses, listening while they plan the demise of a currently unnamed enemy.

I curl my hands around my baby and close my eyes, trying to tune them all out, but when a warm hand covers mine, I snap my eyes open again to find Rio—of course, who else would dare to touch me in his presence?—staring down at my bump with curiosity.

"Is he kicking again?"

"He, or rather, *she*, is being quiet for now," I say. At the flare of concern that flashes across his face, I shake my head. "All good. She's always quiet at this time of the evening. She'll arc up as soon as I lie down to sleep."

"Or *he*."

I release a half chuckle, unable to believe I can actually share a moment of mirth while in a room full of murderers and criminals. But the moment seems strangely intimate, and when he finally grunts and removes his hand, I almost reach out to drag him back.

Eventually, the roundtable breaks up, and drinks are served at the far end of the room. People shear off into groups of two or three, and the chatter grows louder. One of the men —I think he might have been the one named Enzo—makes a beeline for me, but Rio takes my arm and draws me aside, cutting off the man's path and making it clear that any conversation with me is off-limits.

"Scared of what I might say, Rio?" I ask, only half teasing.

He pushes a lock of my hair back off one shoulder before

leaning down to murmur in my ear. "I am always unsure of what you might say or do, little bird. But you performed well just now. I may decide to reward you later."

I arch a brow, daring to push him a little further given his obvious good humor. "I barely did anything, except show up. What was the point of showing me off like that? I was clearly not expected to contribute to the discussion at all. Was it just to show everyone that I am a meek little lamb, back under your control once again?"

"You, a meek little lamb?" His lips lift. "No, Bianca. No one sees you in that light. Least of all me. You are, however, *mine*. And I wanted to remind every single one of the very powerful men in this room that if anyone moves against you, they move against *me*."

*You are mine.*

Unexpectedly, the words send shards of desire shivering through my body, and I'm reminded immediately of the moment when I first sat down here at the table and he grazed my mound. In full view of these men. And how much I wanted him to stretch just that little bit farther with his fingers...

He seems to have an uncanny ability to ascertain my thoughts. His grin this time is wide and wolfish with most of his teeth displayed. "Are you missing my touch, Bianca? Do you want your husband's flesh sunk deep inside you, coaxing you into an earth-shattering orgasm?"

I fold my arms across my stomach. Underneath the fabric of my dress where it rubs enticingly against my breasts, my nipples harden into aching points. "I don't know about earth-shattering, Rio. That's debatable, really."

"Oh, really?" He chuckles, the sound floating around me

like a taunting lilt. "I promise you, Bianca. If I decide to give you an orgasm tonight, it *will* be earth-shattering."

I'm still trying to formulate a response when he signals a couple of the goons to come forward. "Escort my wife back to her suite. Her business here is concluded."

He turns away, effectively dismissing me, and I lean in and tap him on the back. "That's it? Seriously? You're just... done with me?"

His head tilts, but he doesn't turn. As if I'm not worth the effort.

"For now," he says, still facing away from me. "But if I do decide to come for you, be assured any orgasm you achieve *will* be the most earth-shattering you have ever experienced, *mia cara*."

---

### Rio

I MAKE the rounds of the room in the aftermath of the meeting, chatting individually to each of the family heads and trying to focus on business rather than the sexy woman who will likely be waiting for me in her suite. Waiting, and wondering if I will visit her and give her the relief she craves.

*Will* I visit her tonight? I haven't yet decided. Her frustration will grow if I stay away, as will her need. Knowing she wants me, and making her wait until a time of my choosing to give in to her body's pleasure, is a form of aphrodisiac in itself.

But I am punishing myself as much as her with the abstinence, and I am not certain I can go another night with my balls aching, my sheets tangled from the tossing and turning, and my brain not focused where it should be.

On the enemy who threatens us all.

Like me, the others I've invited here are worried, though none of us wish to show it. A visible display of weakness in our world is tantamount to throwing down the gauntlet.

*Here. I am weak. Come take my empire. Come take everything of value to me.*

And so, we all posture and pretend to have things under control. When the reality is, a stranger has clearly entered our midst and is shaking things up. And none of us have a damn single idea who it is or how to stop them.

At least now, we will all be on the lookout for anything unusual, and the lines of communication between us have been reopened. So, the enemy is no longer facing one family alone. He is facing every family in the Northeast of the country combined.

Rossi sidles up to me, a cigar in one hand and a tumbler of whiskey in the other. Part of me is annoyed that he's adapted so well to losing the finger.

"It will be difficult for anyone to move against us now that everyone's eyes have been opened. Clever of you, Rio, to unite the families. But a word of caution. Your father tried the same, a few months before he died."

My mind skitters away from thoughts of Bianca, and I focus on Rossi. He takes a tiny step back under my sudden, intent regard. "My father wanted to unite the families? I was never made aware…"

"You were young. No one thought you would last in the role, so no one thought to apprise you of everything that had happened in the lead-up to your parents' deaths."

"And yet here I am, more than ten years on. Still in the

role, and stronger than ever. Perhaps it is time I *was* apprised, Rossi, of everything you know. Because if not…"

This time, when I trail off, Rossi doesn't provide an answer. He simply nods, the flare of fear noticeable in his expression, before he lifts his tumbler to his lips to drain the contents in a large, convulsive gulp.

Several hours later, the guests finally depart. I intend to go straight to my suite to consider what I have learned this evening and grab a few hours of sleep before the show starts all over again in the morning.

But instead, I find myself taking the elevator down to the bunker where Bianca is living. At least down here, I know she and the baby will be as safe as they can be. This level is strong enough to withstand explosions, and there are limited ways in and out if anyone tries a targeted attack involving guns.

Part of my reason for locking her down here is punishment, of course, but equally, the intention is to keep her safe.

If I had not already forgiven her for running, she would not be here. I have her family fortune; she signed everything over not long after our marriage. I do not need her alive for anything other than personal reasons. And yet, somehow, in the space of several months, she has turned my world and my beliefs upside down.

I can no longer comprehend a world without her in it. Which is problematic in itself, given she ran because she could not conceive of a way to live, and survive, in my world.

We do not fit together in any way, shape, or form.

But I don't care. I will never give her up. Especially not now that she's carrying my child. For better or worse, we are a family, and she will never escape me again.

13

---

*"Hope is the thing with feathers that perches in the soul. "*
Emily Dickinson

*Bianca*

I WAITED hours for Rio before coming to the realization that he had no intention of visiting me tonight. He's a bastard, for sure, and now that I've given up waiting and curled up in bed in my sexy nightie, I'm tempted to reach down between my legs and give myself the earth-shattering orgasm he promised me.

Only problem is, I know it won't be the same unless he's here.

*Fuck him.* He doesn't own my body.

But as soon as I slip a finger into my already-wet seam and swipe around my clit, I still. It's not right. Even though I'm dying to relieve the pressure cooker of sexual tension that grips my body, something feels wrong about doing this without him.

I groan in frustration and thrash my head back against the pillow, but I remove my hand and roll over onto my side to curl up my legs.

The fire and need in my veins stop me from sleeping until somewhere near dawn, if my bedside clock is accurate, and when the housekeeper arrives with my breakfast, she has to shake me awake.

I blink at her before coming awake properly and accept the tray she hands me. As usual, it contains a blueberry muffin and a mug of tea, which has become my beverage of choice at present. Coffee has a bitter, almost metallic taste that it never had before, and I'm hoping that once I've had the baby, my taste for coffee will return. Even the smell of it puts me off these days.

But alongside the muffin is a not-so-usual addition on the tray—a gold-edged white card. An invitation to join Rio on his yacht for lunch and an afternoon on the water. I throw the invite down, tempted to send an answer back upstairs confirming he can go to hell. I wonder who he needs to impress this time. More Mafia gangsters? People in positions of power who have become corrupt over time and are now on Rio's payroll?

Will this be our life from now on? Me stuck down here in my lonely dungeon, summoned when he needs to remind the world he's married, and then shoved back down here far beneath his estate to be forgotten about until the next time he needs to show me off?

But in the end, I decide not to be childish. The invitation provides an opportunity to get away from the estate for a short time and get some fresh air and sunshine on my face. It is likely far too hot up there in the real world, being the end of summer, but the outing hopefully will break up the monotony of my new existence for at least one day.

I only hope Rio gives me the chance to sit out in the sun before he shuffles me back down here to my dungeon.

---

WHEN THE GOONS escort me out across the lawned area of the property and down to the river dock where Rio's yacht is moored, I lift my face to the sun, enjoying the heat on my cheeks.

God, I never thought I'd miss fresh air so intensely. Even with the two short walks I've been allowed each day, it doesn't seem enough.

Luckily, I've chosen a lightweight, floral-patterned sundress featuring a flared skirt that finishes at my knees. I wasn't privy to the weather up here, but I've guessed correctly. Boston in summer is hot, so it didn't really need a lot of brain power to figure it out.

One of the goons guides me up a small ramp onto the yacht itself, and I make a mental note to ask his name when he comes back to collect me. The other regular one, too. It's not their fault they work for a monster. And not all of Rio's men are heartless. Well, I guess maybe they probably are, but I don't like to think of being surrounded by men who murder others simply because they're ordered to.

Rio, on the other hand, is the one who *gives* the orders. So technically, his shoulders are the ones who bear the weight of responsibility for decisions like those. The goons are just the messengers.

The yacht appears to be empty as I reach the deck. I turn

back and frown down at Goon One, who has folded away the boarding ramp and doesn't seem to be following me aboard.

"Where is everyone? Isn't there a party or event or something that Rio wants me to attend?"

Goon Two steps up beside One and shrugs. "We were told to deliver you here, at this time. So that's what we've done, ma'am." He looks past me, over my shoulder, and bows his head deferentially. "Hello, Boss. Do you need anything else?"

"Not at present."

I whirl at the familiar voice to find Rio leaning in the doorway of the captain's area. He's wearing lightweight black trousers and a casual short-sleeved black shirt, and I gape at the unexpected and wholly sexy sight. Other than when we've made love and lain tangled naked in each other's arms, I have never seen Rio dressed in anything other than business attire.

"What's the occasion?" I manage after a pause, when it becomes apparent he's not going to speak first.

"I took the afternoon off."

Can I gape any harder? I think not. "*You* took the afternoon off? You never do that."

He grins then, only a small one, but it transforms his serious features into an expression of utter beauty. My breath stutters and stalls in my throat.

"And yet here I am," he says. "Playing hooky. With you."

Is he trying to flirt?

I step forward, taking his hand when he stretches it out toward me. "I don't understand, Rio. I thought… I mean, are there more people you want to show me off to? Where are they?"

He shakes his head. "Not today. Today it is you and me. I

have some things to tell you, and your doctor was quite insistent I start letting you out for more fresh air and sunlight."

"Oh. This is to help the baby. Of course." The reason for this trip suddenly makes sense.

"No. Not just for the baby, *mia cara*."

"Oh." I must sound stupid, repeating the same word, but he's thrown me off guard with his unexpected warmth and the casual look.

I don't recognize this version of Rio Agosti. He isn't acting at all like an unfeeling mob boss. He doesn't *look* like a mob boss in that open-necked shirt and with his dark hair lifting in the slight breeze that drifts across the deck of the yacht.

"We have a skeleton crew on board today, and security, of course," he says. "But other than that, we'll be alone for the duration of our trip."

"Okay." It's amazing how quickly I've become accustomed to the security tagalongs. This time round—post-betrayal, so to speak—I haven't been given the opportunity to get out and about. But the presence of Rio's security detail on board today is strangely comforting rather than confronting. "Do you still have Danelli in charge of—"

"Danelli is the best *consigliere* in the business. He is loyal to a tee, and I will likely always have him in charge of my security, Bianca." He frowns slightly as if considering what he's just said. "In charge of *our* security."

*Our* security? I like the sound of that.

"Good." I mean it, too.

Danelli and his team may not have saved Francine and those of Rio's staff who died, right here at the estate, but that was only because Rio's second was with us in the club, shooting to kill and keeping Rio and me alive amidst the hail of bullets that surrounded us. No one, not even Danelli, is superhuman enough to be in two places at once. And, given what happened, I suspect he is unlikely to ever slip up again.

If he does, he knows Rio will kill him.

"So, we're going on a trip today? Just you and me?" And our goons. And the team who sails the boat—the team who are even now scurrying about and readying to leave the dock. The vibration of the boat's engine reaches up from beneath my feet. Just another day in Mafia land, where we are never really alone. "What's the occasion, Rio?"

He is still holding my hand and, instead of answering immediately, he tugs to lead me up the stairs and onto the top deck. The sun is hot—I haven't been outside for some time, and up in Cleveland, the heat felt different to this. Less intense. Or maybe it's simply because my pregnancy is progressing, and I feel the heat more keenly now. Still, once atop the stairs, there's a strong breeze blowing that breaks up the heat, and I cross to the railing and lift my chin, watching the passing scenery as the boat begins to head downriver.

Rio stands close—so close the heat from his body wraps around me like the hug of a weighted blanket.

"I wanted to spend time with you away from the estate," he says, finally answering my earlier question. "You've caused me a lot of angst, Bianca, in trying to work out what to do with you without losing face among my people. We are a family now, and we need to decide how we deal with that from this point forward."

I turn to face him, expecting he might step back a touch. But he doesn't. He moves into my space, right up against my belly, and places his hands on the rail each side of me. I am cocooned in his embrace. I look up into his eyes and read desire simmering away in their depths.

The same desire I feel every time I think of him. Every time I see him. The attraction is obviously strong, but he's still the head of a criminal organization, and his world is just as dangerous as it always was.

"You know why I ran. Don't you?" I lay one hand on his chest. Beneath my palm, his heart beats fast, and mine speeds up to match. "Nothing's changed, that I can see. I'm afraid for our child, Rio. Afraid of the violence that will likely color most of his or her life. It seems to be an inevitable thing in your world. And I don't know how to reconcile that with the hopes and dreams I had for my future. How do we keep our baby safe?"

He covers my hand with his. "This is your world too, *mia cara*. I cannot promise that violence will not rear its ugly head. Likely it will. There is a possible war brewing, as you heard in that meeting. I suspect death is coming for more than one of the people in that conference room last night."

I snatch my hand back from beneath his, and turn to face the water, away from him. Those watchful eyes are too deep, too complex. Too knowing.

"Why did you want me there? Was it truly just to show them all that I am back under your control? That you still own the Carlotti cartel as well as the Agosti one? They already know that, Rio. I didn't need to be there."

"That was part of it. But it was also because you *are* mine, and that means you are never getting away from this life. Even if you try. And so, Bianca, you need to understand the stakes, and to know the type of danger that may wait in the shadows. I kept you sequestered from everything last time. And I have kept you down in your...dungeon, as you call it, though I prefer to think of your suite as a safe space for you rather than a prison cell.

"But that situation cannot continue. You are my wife, and you are having my child, and I want the world to see us united as a family. I need you on my side. I cannot fight on two fronts at the same time—against you, and against nameless enemies in the outside world—because then I cannot focus on either. And that is what may get us all killed."

The brown water of the river swirls below the bow of the yacht, reminding me of the day after our wedding. I looked down at those murky depths and considered jumping in to escape him.

I would not have gotten far. Most likely I'd have hit a rock on the river floor or broken my neck or something.

I lift my chin into the breeze, closing my eyes for a moment and enjoying the warmth of sunlight on my face. So much has happened since that day. Good and bad. But I am grateful to be alive, and glad I took the path I did, because it has resulted in a new life being created inside me.

I cradle my belly, feeling a wave of thankfulness that should be at odds with my captive situation. But I cannot be anything but thankful that I've been blessed with the possibility of becoming a mother.

Movement catches my gaze when I open my eyes again, and I watch as a bird dives down beneath the surface and then rises, flapping away with something triumphantly held in its beak. Kill or be killed. It is everywhere, even in nature.

"Do you love me, Rio?" I ask, not sure why that particular question comes out. Why I need to know the truth about how he feels. "I mean, do you *really* love me? Or am I still simply a valuable possession, even now when you already have my inheritance and you no longer need me for that?"

Strong hands grip my shoulders, and he spins me around,

steadying me when I sway a little at the sudden movement. "I do, little bird."

He spears me with the intense look that, in the past, frightened me. I always thought he was trying to decide whether I would live or die when he stared at me like that.

Now, in a flash of awareness, I realize it is simply reflective of the way he lives his life. Intense and passionate, but most of that intensity held tightly beneath the surface so it bubbles there in a whirlpool of fire without ever breaking free.

Is that why the darkness sits so firmly inside him? Is it because he has never had an outlet to release it?

He shakes me slightly, as if aware that my thoughts have wandered. "I never thought I had it in me to love someone to this depth, Bianca. I do not believe I will ever love another, the way I love you. You drive me to distraction, and when you ran, my love turned to hate. I was *murderous*."

His eyes flash, and I flinch, seeing the rage that still lies beneath his smooth words. "But even if you stood in front of me in that moment, I like to believe I would not have harmed you. I can, and will, do whatever is needed to maintain control and protect my family and the organization I run, but you…"

He places a finger beneath my chin, tipping up my face to his. "You are my weakness, *mia cara*. The one chink in my armor. And yet, I can never, ever give you up."

He's about to kiss me. I see it in the tightening of his expression, the focus zeroing in on my lips. And I want him to, more than anything. But I have to speak up first. Somehow, I find the strength to twist out of his grip and put a few feet between us. Only then do I turn back to face him. He studies me with a faint frown, as if I've surprised him, and he can't quite decide how to react.

"I will stay with you, Rio. Because I love you. Insanely, and even when I know you're not good for me. It's toxic, I think, what you and I have. And yet, for better or worse, I can't change how I feel. But…"

I swallow hard and finish quickly before I completely lose my nerve. "I have conditions, and I want you to agree to them before I promise to stay."

## 14

*"When someone shows you who they are, believe them the first time."*
Maya Angelou

*Bianca*

HIS MOUTH PARTS SLIGHTLY, and I hear the sharp intake of breath. Yep, this time there's no doubt about his reaction.

I have definitely shocked Rio into silence.

He gathers his composure instantly, and that unreadable implacability returns to his previously softened features. "Conditions? You expect me to fulfil *your* conditions?"

I straighten my shoulders, trying to see my husband in the man in front of me, and not the scary Mafia boss. "I do."

"And what might those conditions be, Bianca?"

A male waiter tops the stairs and starts toward us with a tray of food, but Rio waves a hand in a violent gesture. The man stops then scurries away to the far corner of the deck. There's a table and chairs set up beneath a shade-cloth awning, and the waiter busies himself unloading the tray there instead.

"Well?" Rio says, forcing my attention back to him.

His voice is soft, but the edge tells me the softness is deceptive. I may be pushing too hard.

I don't care. This has to be said, and if it results in him locking me back up in the dungeon again, then I'll kick and scream and carry on until he has to let me out.

*Or until he decides to kill me*, a traitorous little voice whispers.

But he loves me, and he is already making allowances for me that he won't ever make for anyone else. I didn't know that for sure until today.

"I want you to consider transitioning your business to include legal activities," I state, aiming for a firm tone and annoyed with myself when the words come out in a trembling rush.

Whatever he expected from me, it wasn't that, and he laughs roughly before running a hand through his dark hair, mussing up its usual neatness.

"That's your trade-off for staying with me? It is one hell of a large and difficult condition to achieve, Bianca."

"I know." What I'm asking him is impossible. I want it, so much, but deep down, I know it is simply a pipe dream. "And there's more."

His brows rise. "It's you. Of course there's more."

I cross my arms over my chest, feeling the baby kick suddenly, as if our child is trying to join the conversation. Rio couldn't see the kick, not beneath my sundress, but it is as if he's so tuned in to my body that he knows anyway. His gaze drops to my belly, then rises again. This time, his expression holds a touch of humor.

"Well? What is the rest, then, dear wife? Should I cease calling you little bird and now call you my little moral compass instead?"

"I could live with that." I take a deep breath and release it in a slow exhale. "I also want you to consider funding the Animal Paws Rescue Center, where I used to work." I hold up a hand to cut him off as he opens his mouth. "Not a one-off donation, but as an ongoing thing. Where you become a regular and continuous source of funding for them. You ruined the lives of several of my friends and colleagues when you kidnapped me at their door. It's the least you can do, Rio. *Please*."

I don't mean to add the plea, but I've had a lot of time on my own down in the dungeon to think recently, and I really want to help them in some way. I burned my bridges when I met with Dave and showed so clearly that I love Rio, despite his sometimes-violent lifestyle and despite the fact that his men shot two of my friends. So, I can never go back there to work. But the least Rio and I can do, as a couple, is to donate some of our money to help them.

The Carlotti inheritance was mine, after all, and even though I never knew about it until Rio told me it existed, I should still have the opportunity to spend at least a little of it in ways that I choose.

He breaks into a full belly laugh, the sound so rare and beautiful that my lips automatically lift. Then I realize he's probably about to shoot down my idea in flames, and my smile dims.

But instead of answering my questions, he gestures toward the table where the waiter is still lurking in the corner.

"Come, Bianca. Let's eat. I have something to tell you that might change things for you."

"Will you at least think about—"

"We will eat, and then I will tell you about my little surprise, and then we will talk some more about your…conditions."

That's obviously the best I'll get from him. I didn't really think I could just demand a man like Rio go legit, and he'd say yes and fall into my arms in a happily ever-after situation. Or at least, the logical, reasoning part of me didn't think that. But a tiny voice in the back of my mind keeps whispering.

*You* did *think that, and when he won't deliver, you know you're going to have to run once again. Not now maybe, but one day.*

But I already know that if I try to run for a second time, I won't succeed. He won't let me. And if I attempt it, I'll likely end up dead. No matter how much Rio loves me.

---

*Rio*

WE EAT while the yacht meanders down the river and out into the harbor. I have paid to ensure we are left alone for our jaunt before we head back up the river again. I do not wish to be disturbed.

My orders to Danelli were clear. Do not allow anyone to come near the yacht this afternoon.

The lunch is finally cleared away, the waitstaff has disappeared below deck as ordered, and I lean back on the cushioned seat, studying Bianca. Her dark hair is loose, long locks lifting gently in the breeze that sweeps across the deck. Her cheeks are pink, and the faint sprinkle of freckles across her nose is more pronounced today than usual. She is wearing no makeup that I can discern, and yet, in this moment, she looks more beautiful than I have ever seen her before.

Until she turns those intriguing amber eyes my way and narrows them as if annoyed.

"Well, Rio? We ate. You said you had a surprise to share, and then you would consider my conditions."

I tilt my head. "No. I said I had a surprise for you, and then we would talk."

"Hmm." Even her irritated grunt sounds sexy to me. Everything about her is sexy. "Your surprise?"

"Yes. Come here." I tap the cushion beside me. I want her close when I tell her what I've arranged.

She studies my fingers on the cushion, then shrugs and rises from her spot, repositioning herself beside me. She is sometimes an obedient wife—and yet I love the fact that I never know which Bianca I will get at any given moment.

I lean in, and her delicate perfume wafts up and around me. I am not sure if it is her shampoo or her body soap, or if the scent is purely her, but my senses soak it in as if she is wearing the heady perfume of life itself.

Heady indeed for someone like me, who mostly deals in death.

"I am not going to become a source of income for the Animal Paws Center, Bianca."

"Oh. Right." She starts to wrap her arms across her front, a gesture I recognize as self-protective.

I stop her, grabbing one of her hands and holding it captive in both of mine. "I can offer a better option. I have already put things in motion with my lawyer to set up a new animal rescue center here in Boston. I have purchased land adjacent to the estate. The center will have you at its helm. If you wish. If not, then we can put someone else in to—"

"*No!*"

I blink at her vehement denial. That was not what I expected.

"I mean, no, don't you *dare* put anyone else in to run it. And *yes*! Thank you! That is wonderful news, Rio. When…is this because… No, you said you'd already put things in motion. So, it was before today. Oh, I'm babbling! That's great news!"

She jumps up and then slides onto my lap to hug me.

My cock instantly hardens as her spread pussy presses against me. It is as if my organ has a mind of its own. It gets near her and jumps to attention whether I want it to or not.

I sense the moment she realizes how ready I am by her sudden stillness. Slowly, she lifts her head and stares into my eyes, her own turning a darker shade of honey as her pupils dilate. Her tongue comes out to lick her bottom lip, and then her teeth briefly worry at that same lip before she notices me watching the action.

"You had that planned before today? Before…last night?"

"I called Carnarvon the first week of your return to request he commence negotiations to purchase the land. The property will be big enough to house such a center, without a doubt."

"My first week. When I was down there, underground, railing against you and…you were planning this. For *me*?"

"Of course for you. Such an endeavour would never be something I'd choose for me." The thought is so ludicrous I almost laugh. "Although…" I shrug, trying to tease her a little. I am not used to teasing, and it feels…*good*. "Now that you want our organization to become legit, I may need to call upon my little moral compass to come up with other legal business ideas in which to channel our money.

"Mind you, they will need to be business ideas that make a lot of money in their own right. A shipment of weapons, for example, has an extremely high profit margin. I cannot believe an animal rescue center will yield the same financial gain."

Bianca laughs softly, the sound moving through her body in a vibration that places more exquisite pressure on my cock. "Not unless you're good at applying for government grants. It may well operate at a loss, to be honest."

I mock-frown, enjoying this teasing business. "I do not need to hear that, little bird."

"Oh Rio, you have no idea how happy that idea makes me. How...hopeful..." She leans back in my lap, as if she needs the distance between us to study me properly, and then leans in again.

I cup her cheeks and guide her face close to mine. "I am going to make love to you now, wife. No punishment. No rules or conditions. Not fucking and not sex. We will *make love*, and remind each other what it is like to be unable to keep our hands off one another. Do you want that, *mia cara*? Do you want that as much as I do?"

She doesn't answer. Instead, she simply closes the final bit of distance between us and claims my mouth with hers, about one millisecond before I do the same to her.

## 15

---

*"Love has the power to make a dead heart beat again."*
Wrushank Sorte

*Bianca*

HE CLAIMS my mouth in a kiss, or maybe I claim his. I'm not sure of anything now, except the fact that the man I desire above all else has his arms wrapped around me, his cock hard and ready between my legs as I straddle him, and his tongue teasing mine in a parody of what I want him to do to me down below.

I grind my sex against his flesh. Wanting more. Needing more. Needing to be closer even than this.

I moan, and he swallows the sound and then groans himself, the sound heading straight back into me and down my throat. His groan rips through every cell in my body and inflames my need even further.

I have to feel him inside me. There is no way I can wait a moment longer for Rio.

He cups my hips and holds me steady, encouraging my grind but controlling what would otherwise be a frenzied movement back and forth. I break free of the kiss and arch my back, my head dropping back as I offer him my breasts through the dress.

I assume there'll be people occupying the buildings and apartments and factories that line the river, many of whom can probably see us as we sail on by. I don't care. This is my husband, and I want him to make love to me.

*Not sex. Not fucking. Making love.*

Rio's muscles flex beneath me, and he stands, bringing me up with him with seeming ease despite the extra weight I'm carrying. He slides his hands underneath my ass cheeks, his finger tips dancing along my seam in a teasing caress. I am wet for him, and I'm sure he can feel the damp heat through my panties. I wrap my legs around his waist and cling tightly to his neck as he carries me downstairs and into the cabin below.

He places me on my feet on the luxurious rug and turns toward the large, soft couch. I lament the distance between us, but before I can lunge forward and pull him back to me, he has adjusted the cushions to make space on the couch, then turns back to face me.

With one smooth maneuver, he bends, lifts my dress up and over my head, and then hooks his fingers into my panties and rips them in half. I gasp at the violence of his action, but it ramps up my desire tenfold.

"Better," he growls, then falls backward onto the couch, dragging me with him. "Now you may straddle me properly."

I position a knee each side of his thighs on the couch and

prepare to grind on the bulge in his trousers, but then pause. "Unfasten your trousers, Rio."

"You're commanding me?"

"I am. Do it." Then I spoil the effect by adding, "*Please*?"

To my surprise, he does as I ask, also removing his shirt at the same time, and his huge and ready flesh springs free.

A strangled gasp escapes me. I imagined this very scenario in the dark and lonely moments of the night in Cleveland; his beautiful tanned chest beneath my exploring fingertips, the hard heat of his cock sliding into my ready channel. The erotic dreams staved off the loneliness so many times.

And now he's here, beneath me, and it's all real. The scent of him, the sound of his groan as I flick a fingernail over one of his tight little nipples. The musky, sexy smell that is all Rio lifts up into the air, surrounding me.

I sink down onto his flesh, allowing him to guide me, pausing as the head of his organ breaches me, and sighing in utter bliss when he slides all the way in. "It feels so good, Rio. So good."

"*Fuck.*"

"Fuck…good?" I can't articulate more than that.

I rock my pelvis, and he thrusts upward, his flesh gliding back and forth inside me as if we fit perfectly.

"Fuck, it's *fucking* good." His words are strangled, his voice hoarse, and I begin to move faster, the knowledge that he is as affected by this as me sending me soaring close to the edge almost immediately.

It won't be long, not this time. And as I rock and ride my husband, I beg him to let me come.

"Please, Rio. Please. I can't bear to hold back any longer. Please…"

"Yes, Bianca. Yes! Come. *Now*! Right *now*!"

The order bursts out of him, and I let myself fall, exploding into a million pieces, screaming out as I come around his cock. His roars fill my ears, and his hot seed spills inside of me, and I fall forward against his chest and lose myself in the brief unconsciousness of pure ecstasy.

---

SOMETHING CHANGES between Rio and me on the yacht, and it isn't the fact that he has done something I know is completely out of character and gifted me the opportunity of building an animal rescue.

Nor is it the fact that our lovemaking has become exactly that. Making love, as he said. Not fucking. Not anymore.

The change comes from something deeper, more fundamental, than either of those things. Something at my core that recognizes that, for better or worse, we are meant to be together for however long we have in this world.

I married him because he gave me no choice. I fell for him against my will, calling it Stockholm Syndrome in my thoughts to make sense of the push-pull, love-hate connection. But the truth is more basic. We were enemies, opposites in every way. It didn't matter. We fell in love. Neither of us expected it, but it happened.

I don't know how this is going to play out in the future, but I have to stay and try to make it work. And if I can be his moral compass, in any way, then I will. He joked about that, but I will take it as my mission to subdue that darkness inside of him.

If I can. If it is possible in this Mafia world in which we inhabit.

When we return from the yacht trip, I assume I'll be sent back down to my dungeon. But that isn't the case. While we've been out on the water, rediscovering each other in a physical way, Rio has had my things brought up from below and placed in the suite next to his on the upper floor of the estate.

The connecting door between our suites remains open, and I am happy with that arrangement. At least for now. I want to see if it is possible for us to live more like a real husband and wife, or if this boating afternoon we've just had, away from everyone else, was simply a beautiful anomaly that can't be sustained.

Over the next several weeks, he is away from the estate during the day, presumably attending to business in the city, but at night, he returns and is an attentive husband. We make love most nights when I'm up to it, and on those nights when the tiredness of my advancing pregnancy hits, I curl into his arms and sleep, feeling loved and protected when he holds me.

As my time for the birth draws closer, I ignore the niggles of fear that rise up from time to time, telling myself that if any external threat were to appear, Rio will take care of it. I've been privy to several meetings by now, never with all the heads of family together, but usually with at least one or two in attendance at the estate.

I know they are all searching for a man named Antonio. A man who has made life difficult for several of the Mafia families in recent months. Though apparently, since the heads-of-family meeting, the attacks on various businesses seem to have died off.

Maybe he's been scared away, and everything will finally settle down for a while?

I'm not sure if my blinkered approach is normal for late pregnancy, when the external world fades and focus reduces to nesting and preparing for my child to arrive. Though in truth, it is hardly me doing the nesting. I may have been the one to choose the furniture and décor, but I have an army of people who actually carry out the work to set up the nursery and recreate the vision I have in my head for my baby's space.

The nursery is neither blue, nor pink, but rather a neutral base with a range of colorful pieces to give the room life and joy. I still have no idea if I'm carrying a boy or a girl, but the gender doesn't matter to me. As long as my baby is healthy, I will be happy.

Rio insists we are having a son. I hope he won't be disappointed if the child is a girl. I need him to love this child as much as *I* already do. As the Carlotti-Agosti heir, the child will likely wield enormous power one day, and he or she will need the strength and support of their father to protect them, until such time as they are old enough to protect themselves.

I am musing on this thought one balmy evening in the fall, sitting out on the balcony that juts out from our conjoined bedroom suites, and watching the last rays of sun stretch out across the landscape, when the first pain hits.

I bend forward, clutching at my lower belly. "Ah, holy…jeez."

I gasp when another cramp squeezes me, only a minute or two after the first. *It's too early*, my panicked brain screams, but then rational thought kicks back in and I remember it is only days early, not weeks, and this may actually be the real thing.

Rio and I have spoken at length about the labor and birth. He wants me to have the baby here, where he can better protect us, and plans to bring in a whole team of medical personnel the moment we need them.

Another pain squeezes all the way around my lower back and into my abdomen, and then a minute later, another, so powerful it feels like I'm being torn in two.

*Okay*, I tell myself. *Don't panic.* The pain may not be starting off gentle like I thought it would. But having a baby is normal and natural. Thousands, millions... No, *billions* of people do this all the time.

Fuck, it hurts.

It's time.

I head back inside my bedroom and poke my head out into the hallway, where I know at least two of our security team will be stationed. Today it's Mitch and another Leon, though I can't call him that as it reminds me of the one who died, so he's become Lee whenever I greet him.

They both jump to their feet when I start to speak and then groan again. Lee immediately barks something into his mic and goes racing off down the corridor. Mitch watches him leave as if he's annoyed that he got the raw end of the deal.

Then he sighs and heads over to me, though he looks anything but comfortable when he says, "Ma'am. Is there anything I can...err...you know..."

I wave my hand and shake my head no to put him out of his misery.

These are tough guys and not used to dealing with "women's business," as I heard one of them say to the other only days ago.

He retreats with alacrity to his station, and I stagger back into the bedroom and collapse to my knees beside the bed.

This pain isn't fun. And I'm guessing it may only be the beginning of a long few hours.

The message must pass quickly along the chain as Rio comes rushing in only minutes later, dropping to his knees beside me.

"*La mia cara moglie.*" He strokes my back, stiffening when I groan, loudly. "You're in pain."

"You think?" My voice is gruff, and I speak through gritted teeth.

I know he doesn't mean to be obtuse. He's probably as nervous as I am, and though he's the head of a Mafia cartel and probably ordered hits and been responsible for life and death decisions, I can't imagine he's been the support person for someone giving birth before this moment.

He pats my back some more, and if I weren't riding the wave of yet another cramping pain, I'd laugh at the panic I can feel in the too-rapid touch.

"It's okay, Rio," I manage. "I got this."

"Of course you do. You are a Mafia princess, and my wife. Strength is in your blood." The pride in his voice is palpable, and I can't help the smile lifting my lips.

Until the next wave of pain hits, and I smoosh my face into the bedcover.

"The doctor and her team are en route." He's back to panic mode, patting my back so firmly I squirm to get away from his touch. "They will be here within the next few minutes."

"Ah-huh. Okay. Good. *Fuck*!" When the pain subsides, I look up at him. "Thank you. Now, darling husband, can you please stop whacking me on the back, and help me up onto the bed? Maybe arrange for some towels, too. Protect the bedcovers."

"Oh, beautiful wife. Fuck the bedcovers. I'll buy new ones. I'll buy a whole new bed if necessary."

The next several hours are a blur of pain and sheer effort of will. I've seen animals give birth at the shelter, of course, and my respect grows for their stoic silence and efficiency in preserving their energy for when it matters.

Turns out I'm not stoic. I yell and scream and sweat and thrash so much Rio's sole job becomes wiping my brow and kissing my knuckles while telling me how strong I am. Maybe that's the safest thing the doctor can give him to do so he doesn't step in and take over and simply yank the baby out of me.

It shouldn't be possible to push out a human being from that part of a woman's body, but somehow it is, and at eleven minutes past four a.m., exactly three weeks before my twenty-sixth birthday, our beautiful baby girl is born.

And now, this violent Mafia world truly has the means to hurt us.

## 16

*"For all the things my hands have held the best by far is you."*
Anonymous

*Bianca*

WE NAME HER EMILIA, and she is the most beautiful human being I have ever seen. I don't think she looks like either one of us, though Rio says she has my coloring and my feisty nature. My concern that he wouldn't love her as much as he should, because she's female and not the male heir he assumed, lasted about three seconds.

The doctor had him cut the umbilical cord, and for a big tough Mafia guy, he looked hilariously queasy during that act. But afterward, when our daughter was swaddled and he held her in his arms, the expression on his face was priceless.

For the first time ever, there was wonder and true

tenderness in his eyes, and when he shifted his gaze down to me and delivered a tiny smile, a wave of love washed over me.

I made Rio truly happy in that moment.

And I'm not sure anyone else has ever achieved that with him.

I am no longer naïve enough to believe this reprieve from the external world will last, but I will cherish the memory of that shared birth experience forever.

Over the next several weeks, my focus is on Emilia. Learning to breastfeed, which I thought would be instinctive but turns out is far more difficult than I expected. Dealing with the lack of sleep. Venturing out into the extensive estate gardens with Emilia in a baby sling on my chest, being trailed by goons and pretending my life is as normal as any other new mom.

Rio set me up in the suite adjoining his so we wouldn't wake each other at the wrong time, as he often comes to bed late and is up early, and my schedule currently revolves around our daughter.

He immediately brought in a nanny to help me with Emilia, though the whole concept of paying someone to look after your own child is so far removed from my previous existence that I've struggled to let the poor woman do anything. Except change the diapers, and take over one of the feedings at night if I've had less sleep than usual for whatever reason.

When Doctor Conner returns for the six-week post-birth checkup, she professes herself pleased with my progress, and happy with the health and weight of my daughter.

"You are young and fit, Mrs. Agosti. As is your child. Strong genes on both sides, clearly. If you have not already, you may resume normal relations with your husband any time you wish."

"Oh. Well, okay, thank you." Normal relations? I haven't thought about sex since before the birth. It just hasn't crossed my mind with everything I've been learning to deal with. Now that she mentions it, though, the thought of becoming intimate once again with Rio will not leave my mind.

But he remains absent, busy with whatever it is Mafia bosses do at work, and I continue to mostly dine alone, and walk the grounds, and wrestle with Penn, the nanny, over who should do this task or that, when it comes to Emilia.

Two months after the birth, with Emilia asleep upstairs and Penn watching over her, I am sitting in the library reading, when I realize I can't take the isolation any longer. I need to get out, off the estate, even if it is just to visit a coffee shop or go to a shopping mall. Yes, I now have the run of the beautiful estate gardens as well as the house, but I've come to know this space intimately, and I crave somewhere different.

I leave the library and find Lee in the hallway outside, leaning against a wall and studying his nails. He looks as bored as me, though he immediately straightens when I appear and ducks his head deferentially.

"Afternoon, Lee. Can you please get a message to my husband? I'd like to meet with him for a few minutes if he can spare the time. Today, if possible."

"Yes, ma'am. Right away." He presses his earpiece and turns away to speak quietly. A minute or so later, he nods and swivels back to face me. "He'll be available in his office downstairs in half an hour, Mrs. Agosti. I'll escort you then."

I smile my thanks and retreat back to the library. Downstairs? I'm already on the ground level, so he must mean in the dungeons below the estate. Rio seems to be spending more and more time down there. In the past, his office was up on this level.

Should I be worried about Emilia's safety up here?

I add it to the list of questions to ask Rio, and wait for Lee to escort me down to the meeting.

---

*Rio*

BIANCA'S REQUEST surprises me a little, and I wonder what she wants. When she enters my office, I study her carefully, looking for anything concerning. Her features are set in a serious expression, but otherwise, she seems fine.

"Are you well? Is everything all right with our daughter?"

She nods, though she still doesn't smile. "Everything's fine. We're fine. The doctor said we're well, and healthy and strong. All fine."

"Hmm." I stand and step out from behind my desk, then move forward and grab her hands.

I've been avoiding her much of the time since the birth, mainly because I know she's not been up to sex, and every time I get near her, I want to slide my cock inside her and fuck her so hard she screams.

Just the thought of that right now has me hardening in my trousers. The air changes between us, crackling with sudden awareness. She sucks in a tiny breath and snatches her hand back, rubbing the knuckles in a distracted manner. At least I got some kind of rise out of her.

She heads over to the large couch and sits carefully, still rubbing her hand.

After a moment, I follow her, sitting near but being careful not to touch her again. "What is it you want, Bianca?"

"Oh, yes." She shuffles on the couch as if gathering herself and leans forward. "A couple of things. You've given me the run of the estate, Rio, and for that I'm grateful. But I still feel like a caged bird. I can't bear the idea that this confined space is now my whole and only existence. Is there any way you'll give me permission to leave the estate? A couple of day trips into the city? Shopping, coffee, or a walk in a park? Anything really, just to get away from here and feel normal. *Please*."

Does she know what she's asking of me? I have given her more concessions than any other living being. And she's asking for more.

I tap my forefinger against my lips as I consider what to do. Everyone who needs to knows I held her captive down here in the underground bunker. The dungeon, as she calls it. And everyone also knows she is back under my protection, especially now that we have a child together.

Would anyone dare to harm the mother of my child?

The development of her new animal shelter is progressing. Slowly, but there may be opportunities to involve her a little more in that project. Perhaps it may offer some of the outside stimulation she seems to need.

"I'll consider your request," I say, and she flops back against the couch with a loud and dramatic sigh.

It is moments like those that remind me how young she actually is.

"Not a no, then?" she asks at last.

"Not a no."

"Okay, I can live with that. It's slightly better than I expected."

Finally, she allows a smile to take hold. My breath stutters to a stop for a second at the pure beauty that shines through when she drops her guard.

And somehow, my mouth starts talking before my brain can stop it. "I *am* in need of a partner tomorrow evening, at an event being held in Washington. You may attend with me, Bianca."

What am I saying? She asked for a shopping jaunt to the city, and I am granting her an out-of-state trip?

I could take back the offer. By rights, I should. But the joy that lights her face at my words is worth a thousand doubts about the logic of my decision.

She will be on my arm tomorrow evening, instead of my PA, Dana, who grudgingly gave up tickets to her boyfriend's basketball match when I told her I needed a female at the event.

It is almost as if Bianca's mind is in sync with mine.

She frowns and stares at me quizzically. "So, if you needed a partner for this thing, then you must have had someone else already lined up. Who were you planning— *Oh*. Dana?"

Jealousy laces her query.

"Indeed. And before your beautiful, honeyed eyes turn green with envy, little bird, be aware that Dana will be very happy to miss this one. She has a new beau who likes her to go watch him when he plays his sport."

"Oh. Okay. I didn't know she had a boyfriend. That's...nice."

I grunt at the relief in her tone. "There is no need for you to be jealous of other women, *mia cara*. We are married. I would never disrespect you in that way."

Her head tilts to one side. "You would kidnap me, force

127

me to marry you, lock me in a concrete dungeon, but you would never cheat on me?"

"Of course not. And your *dungeon* was hardly concrete. It had wallpaper and luxurious carpet, last time I looked."

I watch the play of emotions on her face as she tries to decide whether or not to become angry.

Humor wins, and she laughs with a self-deprecating air. "I'm beginning to understand a little more. There's a code of honor in this world. Twisted, maybe, but it does exist..."

"You have much to learn, but yes. Honor and respect are important. And you are my wife. My wife and the mother of my child. If you betray me, there will be consequences, as there would be for me if I were to disrespect you. But that will not happen. I will always try to treat you with respect."

"It seems strange to be saying thanks for that, but I can tell you're genuinely trying to be kind. And moral, in your way. So, thank you, Rio."

I don't bother containing my bark of laughter this time. "So, you really are my little moral compass, then?"

She starts, and my brows lift. Surely, she doesn't really see herself in that role? I shutter my expression so she doesn't see the sudden pity reflected there. She will be sorely disappointed if she thinks she can steer someone like me onto a virtuous path.

*Far too late for that, little bird.*

"Do not thank me too soon," I caution. "You do not know what this event entails, Bianca. Nor who will be in attendance. Perhaps you would prefer to remain holed up here at the estate? It is safer here, without a doubt. Far less so once you venture out."

The humor still lingering in her expression dissipates, and a frown takes its place.

I hold up a reassuring hand, guessing where her thoughts have just wandered. "Emilia will be fine. We will leave our daughter at home with the nanny for this one."

"Oh, but—"

"No buts, Bianca. You may accompany me, if you wish, but Emilia stays here. She will be well protected; I promise you that."

Indecision flickers in her eyes before she nods slowly. "All right. I'd like to go to Washington with you. I've been expressing extra milk, so there's plenty to—"

I hold up a hand. "I do not need to know the details. This event will be formal, so dress accordingly. I will send someone in the morning to assist you with getting ready."

When she finally leaves my office, I take a seat back behind my desk, but it is several minutes before I can concentrate on business once again.

Have I just made an error of judgment, trusting her yet again? Will she use this opportunity to betray me? The nature of the gathering, and those who will attend, means there are more than likely going to be federal agents there, as well as rivals who would love to see me taken down.

It is a given that I will have enemies in attendance. More than one. And I need to guard against them.

Last time we attended an event like this, Bianca was accosted in the bathroom by a member of law enforcement. I cannot guarantee they won't try the same thing again. And if it does happen again—or even if Bianca is only *perceived* to be behaving in a suspect way—she is likely to feel the full wrath of the Mafia world come raining down on her head.

Baby or no baby, my wife will not survive if she tries to cross the Agosti family in the future. Even if my love for her blinds me to her faults, and even if I do not have the strength or the will to harm her, there are others within the family and the business who will be at pains to ensure she doesn't see the sun rise the next day.

And then, my darling daughter, Emilia, would have to grow up without her mother.

## 17

---

*"We have true power when we support each other."*
Bert McCoy

*Bianca*

IT BOTHERS ME, leaving Emilia home without me when she's still so young, but I understand why Rio has made that decision. He wants to protect our daughter and doesn't feel like he can keep an eye on me, plus Emilia, as well as conduct whatever business he has in Washington, without something or someone falling through the cracks.

Neither of us wants that "someone" to be Emilia.

When a team of helpers arrives late in the morning to do my nails, hair, and makeup and choose my clothing and jewelry for the evening, I have to confess I'm less surprised than I was the first time that happened. There is something to be said for having the money to afford this level of pampering.

It may feel ridiculous and like a whole lot of overwhelm, but when I have one person styling my hair, another applying skin products and rimming my eyes with perfectly applied liner, and two more buffing my nails and giving me both mani and pedicures, it is hard to summon hatred for the luxurious way of life.

What does surprise me, though, is when a young woman bounces into my suite, her long dark hair falling in an artful sprawl down her back and her chocolate-brown eyes wide with curiosity as she stops and stares at me from partway across the room.

"Bianca? Oh my God, it's so lovely to finally meet you in person!"

She bounds across the rest of the space and comes to an abrupt stop in front of me. I can't get up as my feet are currently soaking in a warm oil bath and my fingernails are drying in a little machine on the table by the side of my chair.

Otherwise, I may have jumped to my feet and given her a spontaneous hug. She gives off that sort of positive energy.

"Hello." I smile and study her curiously, noting a certain familiarity, but I've never met her before. Then it dawns on me who she looks like, and I gape up at her in genuine wonder. "Are you Rio's...sister?"

The same eyes as his blink back at me; the same strong yet refined features. But in this young woman, the rigid implacability that makes up Rio's core is missing. Instead, there's a soft joy in her face, and her wide lips lift in a grin, both cheeky and unaffected.

She squats down by my chair to match my seated height. "Yes. I'm Angelica, though everyone just calls me Angel, and

I want you to call me that, too. I've been in Switzerland, but I've finished school at last. Thank *fuck*! Oops. I'm not supposed to swear here. And now I'm back here to live. I'm sure we'll be good friends, Bianca. Nicky has told me so much about you!"

Nicky? The brother I met at the wedding. Not Rio? My mind is still processing that, but she's waiting for my response.

"I... Ah, I'm very pleased to meet you, Angel. Rio has..."

*Told me nothing about you, except the fact that he's planning to arrange a marriage for you. You should run, little Angel. Back to Switzerland. Have some fun while you still can.*

I tamp down the inappropriate thoughts. "He's mentioned a lot about you," I lie. "And I'm sure we'll be friends, too."

That last part is not a lie. Angel gives off such an energetic vibe, and I instinctively feel happy that she's here.

"I'd get up and give you a hug, Angel, but...*ouch*!"

The hairstylist has tugged at my hair, as if afraid I may actually try to get up. But she did it harder than she needed to, and Angel frowns at the stylist, obviously having noted the act.

"Don't do that again. You'll hurt her," she scolds.

Then she folds her body into the lotus position on the floor in front of me. I'm only twenty-six, but I don't think I have the easy flexibility that Angel displays. How can I suddenly be feeling old at my age?

"When you're done here, will you take me to meet Emilia? I want to be introduced to my gorgeous niece. Oh, I'm so glad you're here, Bianca. I was worried I'd be completely bored to fucking death when I came back.

Surrounded by a bunch of strict old businessmen and forced to sit around and wait to be married off to one of them."

A shocked chuckle rises up my throat at her description. It fits with the truth, and it's sad that she seems to accept that as her lot. Before I can respond, though, Angel continues.

"But Rio said he only had so many eyes and Danelli might be great, but he's not superhuman, and he needed me back here in Boston so his men can keep an eye on me. And keep me safe. Which, apparently, they can't do if I swan around Europe like I planned. I mean, he didn't even want me to go stay with our cousins in Italy. He's a spoilsport. But, you know, *danger* and all."

She does the "air quotes" thing with her hands, obviously expecting me to laugh. But I can't. She's just nailed the underlying theme of this whole family's existence.

Do they know how horrific it is to live their lives always on the edge of danger? An existence in which one wrong step can result in death or harm for the people we love? Or are they all so used to it that it's simply second nature to prepare for the worst?

For the first time, true sympathy for Rio rises in my heart, and I remember with a pang the first time we made love when he brought me back here once again.

The blackness that lurked on the edges of his expression that night, keeping his muscles tense and his hands clenched. And keeping me hovering on the edge of terror even when he was pounding into me with utter desperation.

Does that darkness stem from circumstance? He never had any choice about being born into this world, and as the eldest, he was always going to have the leadership of the family and its organization thrust upon his broad shoulders.

When *my* parents were killed—even though I was too

young to remember it and didn't even know about the situation until recently—I was lucky enough to have someone take me away from this life and give me an opportunity to grow and thrive somewhere normal.

Rio never had the opportunity for normal. Or at least, not as I define it.

When his parents died, did he even have a chance to grieve? Or did he have to put emotion aside so he could step up and take over, accepting responsibility for the sake of this young woman in front of me? And for his younger brothers, Nicky and Luca. And indeed, for everyone in their extended family and on the payroll.

People like Francine. Danelli. Everyone who relies on him.

What if Rio had been born the younger brother? Would he have had a little more of the playful nature that Nicky displayed at our wedding and during the reception? Would he have any of the softness and joy for life that I see in Angel's face right now?

I may not like what Rio is, nor agree with the decisions he makes with regard to his business, but I *can* empathize with the fact that he may be that way because it is the only path in life he was offered.

"I would love to take you to meet Emilia," I say to Angel, realizing that I've hesitated too long. I lace the words with warmth to convey how genuinely happy I am that she's here. "But first, how do you feel about helping me choose a suitable dress for this event I'm to attend with Rio this evening?"

The resultant squeal confirms that Angel does, indeed, wish to help me, and for the first time since Rio fetched me back here from Cleveland, the underlying dread that sits within me begins to ease.

It will be so much more fun having another young woman here to hang out with.

Angel jumps to her feet and rushes over to my dressing room to peer through the assorted dress choices. And even though her presence has lightened my mood, there's still a niggle at the back of my mind I try to ignore.

Why has Rio felt the need to bring Angel back here at this time? Is there a new threat looming that I'm not aware of?

A shiver of foreboding works its way down my spine.

---

"DID YOU ENJOY MY LITTLE SURPRISE?" Rio asks, as the private jet in which we're traveling to Washington prepares to land.

It has taken less than two hours to get here, but every step of the journey has been pure luxury, from the Rolls-Royce that collected us at the estate, and now this leather-seated plane with attentive waitstaff and expensive canapes to keep us from starving to death on the short journey.

"Do you mean Angel?" I can't help smiling at the thought of the young chatterbox. "She's lovely. Will she be living at the estate with us from now on? She mentioned that, but it was amongst a whole lot of other chatter, so I wasn't sure if I'd heard her correctly or not."

"Yes, indeed. Angel talks far too much. That will be a factor in the marriage negotiations, no doubt."

"I… *What*?"

"I have already told you. It is my responsibility to find my sister a husband, but I will need to highlight her attributes to counteract the negative regarding how much she speaks."

I open and close my mouth a few times, unable to think of

anything that isn't either a swear word or an insult to Rio. Every time I start to soften my attitude toward him, he says something that snaps me back to reality.

This male-dominated, misogynistic Mafia world...

Finally, I settle on, "Angel has every right to speak as much or as little as she wishes. I think she's utterly charming. Unlike her brother."

He narrows his eyes, but I'm not finished.

"And she's, what? Eighteen? Honestly, that's far too young to be considering marriage, Rio. Especially if someone else is planning to pick out a husband for the poor girl."

His mouth thins. "Angelica is now nineteen. And she has known about—and accepted—the arranged marriage situation since the moment she could walk and talk. She will be married before she turns twenty-two."

"You can't 'accept' a situation like that when you're just a child barely able to talk. She wouldn't even have understood what she was agreeing to!"

"It is how things are done, Bianca."

"Maybe in your world," I mutter, turning my head to stare out the window.

The lights of Washington stretch out below as far as my eyes can see. Focusing on a place I've never before visited is far preferable than getting into an argument with Rio right now.

Because I know I'm correct, but I cannot win against him. He's so set on tradition, and he believes he is helping his sister toward a better future, not harming her. The frustration roils in my gut, churning up the sparkling water and caviar blinis I've consumed during the flight.

"It's your world, too," he says softly, but there's an edge to his tone that tells me I've riled him.

*Good*. He's riled me up, too.

I am damn sure not letting him do that to our Emilia, though I've got a few years yet to make him change his mind. Maybe I can add that to the list of challenges, the main one being to steer him toward decisions that are less…illegal.

*And pigs might fly*, I think, looking out at the clear and completely pig-less sky.

"Well." I turn back to face him and allow my annoyance to show, flashing him a wide, fake smile. "It's going to be a great night for sure, isn't it?"

"It will be…interesting," is all he says before his expression closes down, and he shifts his attention to a report sitting unread on the fold-out desk in front of him.

"What is it for, this event? Who's hosting it? Is it a fundraiser?"

At first, it seems as if he's not going to answer, and then he heaves a sigh and raises his gaze back to mine. "The event is an engagement announcement for the host's daughter." He bares his teeth at me in a parody of a grin. "For an *arranged* marriage."

"Oh. Great." *Shit*.

"The host, by the way, is Gianni Martelli."

*Double shit*. Everyone has heard that name. He's as infamous in the media as Rio himself. Many years older than my husband, and known to be involved in criminal activity but with apparent Teflon-coated armor. He has a similar reputation for wielding power with an iron fist.

He was the only family head not at the meeting Rio arranged, I remember suddenly, and there was some murmuring about one of Martelli's men possibly being the one involved in the sabotage.

Whether Gianni Martelli is Rio's enemy, or whether they

are in business together, then my hopes of guiding my husband toward a more moral path are useless.

Stupid, naïve, and useless.

It may be easier to try convincing an African lion to become a vegetarian.

## 18

*"You can't get anywhere in life without taking risks."*
Esme Bianco

*Bianca*

I THOUGHT the engagement event would be held at a fancy hotel in one of the more expensive areas of the city, but the Rolls-Royce that collects us at the airport travels north and finally glides to a stop at a grand old home in the Potomac area, according to the signs we pass. The estate reminds me of Rio's, though this one is built in an older style with a cream façade and huge columns that give the place a Greco-Roman feel.

Obviously, we are partying at the Martelli mansion instead of somewhere public. That fact makes me even more nervous than I already was. What if Martelli's security isn't as good as Rio's? What if someone breaks in and shoots us all, like Anders did, and I end up as dead as Francine?

*Stop being silly*, I chide myself. *Rio won't let anyone hurt us.*

I'm surprised to find I actually believe that thought. Mostly.

Funny how I've come round somewhat to trusting my husband with my safety, instead of being afraid of his wrath all the time. There's a sense that Rio's protective instincts have kicked in when it comes to me, and that is definitely the case in relation to Emilia.

The realization that he sees us as worth protecting sends warmth through my body. I cling to his arm when we alight from the vehicle and are escorted into the building by several suited men. Men who don't bother trying to hide their weapons.

I glance around, looking for *our* goons, but can't see any familiar faces.

Rio seems to sense my unease because he leans down to whisper in my ear, "Relax, little bird."

"Is Danelli here? Or his men? Lee? Where are our guys?"

"*Our* guys?" His lips twitch. "I like that you describe them that way. Unfortunately, we have had to agree to leave most of our team at the gate. Danelli has been granted permission to enter, and he is already inside. If he had seen anything untoward, he'd have been in contact already. I have been given assurances by the host that we will be safe here this evening. I would not have brought you here if I did not believe that to be true."

I nod without answering. I am certain *Rio* believes that, but whether I believe the assurances of someone I've never met is a whole other thing altogether. Still, there's nothing I can do except hold tight to Rio, with my hand tucked in the crook of his arm, as we follow others who have just arrived through a grand entrance foyer and into a huge parquet-floored ballroom.

The space is decked out with floral displays and white-cloth-covered tables arranged around a cleared space in front of a small orchestra already playing softly. And in the center of the room's entry, where no one can miss it, is an ostentatious display that features an enormous ice sculpture of a young couple set in a bed of lily-pad-topped water.

Holy hell. This is decadence on a scale I've never seen before.

"The happy couple, I presume?" I murmur to Rio, staring up wide-eyed at the sculpture.

"It is," he confirms, before frowning. "It is *her,* at least," he corrects himself. "The fiancé is a damn sight older than this depiction. *This* looks like the man's grandson."

*Oh.* Before I can process that thought, Rio reaches out and snags drinks for us both off a tray carried by a passing waiter.

There are hundreds of people already milling around, and unlike the last gala event at which I knew only Rio and Carlos Rossi, this time I recognize several faces from the various meetings Rio has allowed me to attend.

And there, finally, I spot Danelli, leaning against a pillar and studying the crowd. He nods at me when I meet his watchful gaze, and the tension across my shoulders relaxes a touch. I may not like what I imagine my husband's *consigliere* does for Rio, but I know he will do his darndest to keep us safe.

I spy a goatee-bearded man who I remember from Rio's estate—I think his name was Darov. The name struck me at the time, as he seemed to be one of the few in Rio's business orbit who doesn't have an obvious Italian background. He's talking with another man I recall from the same meeting— Enzo. That one is definitely Italian. I remember his accent was strong, and I think perhaps English must be his second language.

They and others I've seen at the estate acknowledge me with polite yet dismissive nods, which is about as much as I can expect. This world is not designed for a woman to be seen as anything other than window dressing for their chosen man.

With a start of nerves, I see Carlos Rossi skirting through the crowd over near the other side of the large room. I haven't seen him since that meeting at Rio's, and we barely spoke on that occasion. Will he try and seek me out tonight? The thought sends shards of tension straight back into my system, and my pulse rate speeds up slightly.

Rossi stops short when he sees Rio and me, and something flashes in his expression before the usual bland indifference descends. He mouths something unintelligible that I can't lip read—at a guess, it is some kind of greeting. He follows up with a noncommittal smile before lifting his glass in a salute and then turning away.

I'm clutching my drink and trying to match more names to faces when I sense Rio's intense gaze on me. My cheeks heat when I glance at him and notice the unexpected warmth in his eyes.

He leans in close. "I have been neglectful, Bianca. I should have told you right from the start that you look utterly stunning this evening. Your body has filled out since having Emilia. You are more voluptuous, and that lovely red dress shows off your curves to perfection. The way it drapes down elegantly over your hips almost to the floor—it highlights everything about you that I find desirable. You look good enough to eat, in fact."

*Eat*? The thrum of desire between my legs is instant, and it only ramps up more when he lifts a hand to my face and traces a finger along one of my cheekbones. "Your hair styled up like this is a delightful change. Showcases your bone structure and the delicate line of your neck."

His finger trails down my neck, along my collarbone, and then follows the line of my strapless bodice. I shiver beneath his touch. The caress is featherlight but no less impactful for its barely there nature.

"But I will always prefer you with your hair tumbling everywhere, no makeup, and with your light dusting of freckles on show. Especially when your beautiful mouth wraps around my cock and you stare up at me with that burning need in your eyes. The need you are showing right now, in fact.

"Innocence and sensuality. You offer both in one package, Bianca, and it drives me to distraction far more than it should."

I have no idea how to answer him. And I couldn't, even if the right words did come. He has rendered me breathless.

His thumb drifts across my lips, and I only just hold back the urge to suck in his digit in a parody of what he has just described.

*Not here*, I remind myself. *Not appropriate*. Not among this crowd of murdering vultures.

The pressure of his thumb increases briefly, as if he can sense my hesitance and is daring me to do something risqué anyway.

Then his hand drops away, and he turns to greet someone,

and I'm left with an unfulfilled ache at my core and a growing doubt that the moment of intimacy existed anywhere except in my head.

"Martelli," Rio says smoothly, drawing me in close to his side without looking down at me. Nerves flutter in my belly, washing away any remaining ribbons of desire, and I look up to meet the cold expression of this evening's host. "Congratulations to your daughter, and to your family. You have secured a good match for Daniela."

"Yes, I have, Agosti. A very good match." The voice is low and monotone. Nothing threatening about it whatsoever on the surface.

But the unblinking gaze that accompanies the words, on me rather than Rio who spoke, sends a shiver of trepidation through my body.

Gianni Martelli is Rio's equivalent here in Washington. A mob boss in charge of a large outfit. His powerful energy vibrates around him as strongly as Rio's does. Studying them side by side, I recognize certain similarities in the two of them, but I feel nothing except repulsion for the man whose home we are standing in right now.

It takes a moment to force my voice to work. "Mr. Martelli. Thank you for having us as your guests this evening."

His answering smile reminds me of a snake's smile—and I remember from my animal shelter days that the only reason a snake does that is when it is preparing to bite. "Bianca Carlotti. Your reputation precedes you. How delightful to finally meet you."

I swallow hard and, without meaning to, find myself pressing more firmly into my husband's side. But despite my fear, I feel the strangest urge to push our host.

"I'm not Bianca Carlotti. I'm Bianca Agosti," I correct quietly.

I'm only aware of Rio's faint start because I'm wedged so tightly against him, but that telltale response makes me realize I've possibly made a faux pas in correcting Martelli.

Is one little correction considered tantamount to a disrespectful slap in the face? Surely not?

My heart sinks. What am I doing? Every time I think I know how this world works, the playing field tilts and shifts, only this time when it realigns, I know I've just made myself a powerful enemy.

There's a moment of silence, where everything around me drops away. Is that what real fear does to you? Places you in a bubble of terror that cuts off everything except the impending threat?

Then Martelli chuckles, a thin, fake sound, and the party around us rushes back in.

"Like I said, a delight to meet you." He turns to Rio and nods. "We will talk later, when the formalities of the evening are concluded. Until then, enjoy yourselves. And Agosti, perhaps consider shortening the leash with which you have this lovely creature shackled."

He turns and melts into the crowd before I can even begin the outraged sputter that comes out of my mouth. "My leash? What the actual hell, Rio? *That* is Martelli? He's the rudest motherfu—"

"*Silence*, Bianca."

I blink at the viciousness of his tone and look up into a set of furious dark eyes.

"Remember where we are. Do not antagonize our host. He will likely seek you out later, and when he does, you *must* be subservient. He will push you, looking for weakness, but do not respond with anger. He will be looking at you to find a chink in *my* armor, and we cannot let him find one."

"He has no authority over me. No one does."

"No one?"

"Well." I release a sound almost like a growl at the unjust nature of this situation. "*You* do. I guess."

"You...*guess*? Hmm. We will need to remedy that uncertainty later. In the bedroom, perhaps. I believe it is time to remind you, little bird, who is in control."

The fury in his expression has already faded, and now it is replaced by something else. Desire? Yes, I read that clearly in the depths of those dark eyes. But just before he takes me by the arm and pulls me farther into the crowd, I'm sure I also see a flash of approval.

---

RIO SPENDS much of the evening circulating and conducting quiet, intense discussions that seem to revolve around business. I stand near him, catching bits and pieces of conversation, but the music, laughter, and the crowd's voices serve as an effective screen masking what he's saying. In the end, I give up trying to follow him and start people-watching instead.

A man who looks familiar soon catches my eye. Rio's brother Nikolas. I've only met him once or twice, around the time of our wedding, but like everyone in Rio's family, his charismatic presence is memorable.

When I smile a polite greeting, he makes a beeline for my side.

"How is my favorite sister-in-law?" he asks, taking me by

both of my elbows and leaning in to kiss my cheeks, first one side then the other.

He is so different in manner to Rio, less rigid, and with an edge of humor softening his face and his actions.

I snort at his question and shake my head. "Unless your younger brother, Luca, got married without Rio's knowledge, I think I may be your only sister-in-law."

"Ah, but even if I had ten brothers, all married, you would still be my favorite."

I can't help the laugh that pops out. "Would I just? *Despite* the fact that I tried to run, or because of it, Nikolas?"

I am genuinely curious about what the rest of the family thinks of my escape and subsequent recapture. Rio has made it clear my flight was considered a betrayal of the worst kind, but other than Angel this morning, I haven't seen anyone except goons, medical personnel, and estate staff, so there's been no one other than Rio to gauge family reaction.

He laughs too, a short chuckle that disappears almost as fast as it arrived. "Nicky, please. Never Nikolas. That's far too formal." He pauses to study me before adding in a suddenly serious tone, "And *despite* it, Bianca, not because of it. I might sometimes seem like a lightweight fool when compared to Rio, but I love my brother, and I am loyal to him. I would never condone a betrayal of our family."

A chill unexpectedly runs across my skin, causing tiny goose bumps to rise up on my arms.

"Nicky." I nod to confirm that I'll use the name he wishes. "What would you do if I betrayed Rio again? Not that I'm planning it, but just asking out of curiosity."

His eyes flash, and a rigidity descends across his expression. For a moment, he looks exactly like his older brother. Violent. Implacable. *Dangerous*. "It is my belief that Rio is incapable of harming you, Bianca. He loves you too much, and that concept is new to him. Loving someone simply *because*, and not for family or obligation."

"Simply because?"

"Yes. You are opposites in every way, and yet somehow, you both seem to fit together. No one expected it, I have to admit."

I look across at my husband, still embroiled in a discussion several feet away. We fit together? I like that idea, a lot, even though deep down, a large part of me doesn't believe it to be true.

Then Nicky continues speaking in a conversational tone, and my attention whips back to him when he says, "So, it would fall on my shoulders to kill you, dear sister-in-law, should you step out of line again."

My lips part, and suddenly, I find it hard to swallow.

"Don't make me do that." Between one blink and the next, the violent edge disappears from his features and joviality is back. "I like you. I like your feisty spirit, and I like the fact that your presence makes my brother happier than I've ever seen him." He gives me a pseudo-friendly pat on my bare shoulder, and I shiver beneath the touch even though his fingers are warm.

A death threat from a member of my new "family."

"I will never take you for a fool, Nicky," I finally manage. "Or lightweight."

"Good. Then I think we're going to get along famously. Would you like to dance?"

I shoot another glance at Rio, willing him to look my way. I don't want to dance with Nicky. He just threatened to kill me. As if he senses my distress, Rio looks up from his conversation, frowns when he sees who is standing with me, and murmurs something to his companion before striding over.

"Nicky. I did not expect to see you here. What do you want?" Rio's tone is flat, and his gaze darts between his brother and me as if trying to guess the nature of our conversation.

"I am simply having a friendly chat with your lovely wife."

I step closer to Rio and tuck myself in beneath his arm. The irony of seeking comfort and protection from Rio is not lost on me. Nor on Nicky, it seems, whose eyes spark with obvious humor.

Rio's arm automatically comes around me. I open my mouth to ask him to dance with me so Nicky can't, but the latter steps back and gives a smile and nod that looks to all the world like a normal, friendly, leave-taking.

"Until next time, brother. And new sister." He waggles his fingers and then disappears into the crowd.

It is some time before my heart rate returns to a more normal pace.

And I can't help but wonder if this family I've joined will actually end up being the death of me. Literally.

*"Avoiding danger is no safer in the long run than outright exposure. The fearful are caught as often as the bold."*
Helen Keller

*Bianca*

AS THE EVENING WEARS ON, my breasts begin to ache and, with Rio's permission, I take my leave directly after the speeches. He spears me with an unreadable look, but allows me to leave his side so I can find a member of the host's security detail and let them know my needs. I was told on the way here that a private space to pump milk had already been discussed and arranged—no doubt by the capable and efficient Dana.

It's several minutes before I figure out what that look of Rio's likely meant. He was probably remembering the last time we were at a fancy event like this. I disappeared to the bathroom during a gala fundraiser in Boston, and that's where I met Felicity from the Feds.

Not that I planned that meeting, but Rio must be wondering if something similar may occur tonight. I hope it doesn't. I'm beginning to enjoy my newfound freedom, and I don't want to be sent back to that dungeon prison. No matter how luxurious it is.

And I most certainly don't want to risk being killed by my brother-in-law.

After chatting into his earpiece and mic and ascertaining where to take me, Martelli's security guy leads me down a long hallway to a small sitting room. While I stand in the doorway, the guy checks the room, making certain it is empty and that the curtained windows are properly locked, and then he beckons me in.

I frown when he takes a stance near one of the settees, and I indicate the equipment waiting on the low coffee table. "I'm about to bare my breasts and pump milk with this thing. I don't think my husband, Rio, would like anyone other than him looking at certain parts of my body. Do you?"

"Rio, ma'am? You're…Mrs. *Agosti*?"

I smile sweetly at his discomfort. "I am. And Rio is very jealous, as everyone knows. But I guess you can stay here if you wish, though I can't guarantee what my husband's reaction will be if he finds out…"

He shuffles his feet, glancing at my decolletage then quickly away. "I'll be directly outside the door, ma'am. If you call out, I will be in within seconds."

"That sounds good. Thank you." Maybe I'm better at game playing than I thought.

He rushes outside and closes the door behind him, and I sink back onto the brown leather settee with a sigh of relief.

The weeks in the underground suite were lonely, but I was never really one for partying or nightlife. A good book was always more enticing to me than a nightclub.

I sigh again, enjoying the almost-silence of the room. I can still hear muted sounds floating down the hall from the ballroom, but now they offer a pleasant background noise rather than an unpleasant cacophony.

I'm not too concerned about whatever is going on outside the windows. There are heavy drapes blocking the view, and if Gianni Martelli's outfit is anything like Rio's, the gardens will be swarming with security. Danelli will be out there too somewhere. I am likely as safe in here as I am out there on the dance floor.

I busy myself attaching the pump and let it do its thing, taking the time to think about everything and everyone I've met tonight.

My thoughts drift toward Nicky and then quickly skirt away. For better or worse, he's my brother-in-law, and I will have to get used to his presence.

I consider our host, Martelli. It's pretty obvious that he dislikes Rio. It couldn't be jealousy, though, as they seem to be considered equals in their way. Does he see Rio as a threat to his power base? *Is* Rio a threat? My husband loves Boston, and I can't see him wanting to expand his operations all the way here to Washington.

Though given it's Rio, who knows?

I can only go on instinct, but I can't see that as a reason for Martelli's antagonism toward Rio. If not that, then what is it driving the underlying dislike?

I can't help thinking about the animal world and how that works in comparison to this one. I miss the rescue center so much, even though they're unlikely to ever want me back.

But if I stay with Rio, at least one day I may have a new shelter to help set up and run.

And maybe I can take something of what I learned over the years of working at the shelter and apply it to this crazy Mafia environment. Animals fight because they want to possess or gain something for their survival. Might be food, or territory, or a mate. Martelli definitely isn't after me—not after the first words out of my mouth were a perceived insult. They both have enough money to start a small nation each, so it isn't likely to be that. Territory? Does Martelli want more? Does Rio want more?

What if this elusive guy they're all searching for—this Antonio—works for Gianni Martelli?

Is Martelli hiding him within the ranks somewhere, and Rio hasn't had any luck finding him because he's less familiar with this area and its operations than what occurs in his own city?

The more I consider the idea, the more it seems to crystallize in my mind as a probability. I need to get back to Rio and share some of my thoughts with him.

I finish the pumping, enjoying the relief of emptied breasts, and pack everything away, then reassemble my dress and jump up to head back to the ballroom. I pull open the sitting-room door, expecting to see the security guy who escorted me here. Instead, I come to an abrupt halt at the sight of a tuxedoed man in the act of reaching out toward the door handle.

Gianni Martelli.

He immediately grabs me by my shoulders, shoves me backward none too gently into the room, and steps into the space with me, slamming the door shut behind him.

I catch sight of the security guy's face just before the door closes—startlement that immediately settles into impassivity. Of course. This guy works for Martelli. I am on my own, at least for the moment.

I stare up into the dead-looking eyes of my host and start babbling. "Rio said he'd meet me here. He's overdue. He'll be here any minute. I'm certain of it."

I'm spouting nonsense, and both of us know it.

Martelli smiles that snake smile of his, and my blood runs cold.

"Take a seat, then, Bianca *Agosti*, and we will wait for your husband to arrive." He gestures at the settee I've just vacated, and I slide back down onto the seat before my trembling knees give away my terror.

He studies me for a moment before taking a seat opposite. The low coffee table lies between us, and I can't help my flinch when he leans forward. But he's merely reaching for a cigar box on the table beside the packed-up pump. He busies himself cutting and lighting a cigar, puffing on it before looking at me again.

"I hope you don't mind me lighting up, Mrs. *Agosti*? This is my favorite room in which to enjoy a cigar."

*Of course I bloody mind, you horrible man. I hate cigars. Except when it comes to Rio*, my recalcitrant mind adds. On him, cigar smoke smells delicious. On this man, it makes me want to gag.

I smile sweetly, I hope. It was easy to play a game with one of the goons. They're primed to obey orders, and I *am* a mob boss's wife, after all. Far harder to play a game with someone like Martelli.

"I don't mind," I lie. "And if we got off on the wrong foot earlier, I apologize. I was..." My heart is thumping, and I hope I'm saying the right things and not making the situation

155

worse. "I was just wanting to please my husband, Mr. Martelli. Acknowledge his name. That's all. I didn't mean to cause you any offence. Really, I…"

The steady regard from those cold eyes freezes my voice box. Again. I clear my throat, trying to get it restarted, to no avail.

He puffs away, then says, "Well. Seems your husband is *long* overdue. Though I'm not surprised. The last I saw him, he was having a rather animated discussion with Julia Veneto. They looked to be getting very cozy in one of the alcoves off the ballroom."

*That* kick-starts my voice again. "Julia Veneto, the actress?"

The very beautiful, very sexy, and currently very available Hollywood actress?

"That is the one. Oh dear. What a shame for you, Bianca *Agosti*."

My eyes narrow. Suddenly, I've had enough of him. I don't care how rich and powerful this guy is, nor do I care *what* he is. "The thing is, Mr. Martelli, Rio is my husband. He loves me, and he's loyal. He would never disrespect—"

"Indeed, I would not." I turn to the door, where Rio has just entered.

His eyes are burning with emotion of some kind and, looking at him now, I cannot believe I ever thought him cold.

Not like the man seated opposite. There is no comparison between the two. None at all. I jump to my feet and rush to Rio, my tension dissipating as he wraps strong arms around me. Seeking his protection appears to be becoming a habit.

He may be a violent monster who scares others the way Martelli scares me. But Rio is *my* monster. And right now, I'm so grateful I have him on my side.

"You are...untouched?" He murmurs the words quietly into my ear. So quiet I can barely hear him.

I nod, but I'm certain he can feel my trembling. I don't want anything to start up between these two. Especially not now, when we are smack bang in the middle of Martelli's territory and surrounded by his people.

"I'm good," I confirm. "Milk pumped and in that refrigerated bag ready to take home."

I point at the table, and Rio grimaces a little, but his stance relaxes a touch, and I can tell the underlying anger is abating.

"If you head straight back out to the ballroom, Bianca, there is someone who wishes to speak with you."

"Oh? But what about—"

"Go, *mia cara*. Carlos Rossi is waiting."

My heart sinks. I want to go home, not talk to yet another gangster with a slick and clearly fake surface persona.

"Fine. But is it almost time for us to leave?" My voice comes out smaller than I want.

Rio cradles my cheek. "Soon. And then I believe it will be time to discuss the matter of *control*. Who wields it. And who does not. Would you like that?"

Despite the older man's presence, my insides light up at Rio's promise. "I would love that, *mio caro marito*."

He huffs out a laugh, clearly surprised.

"I asked Angel this morning how to say 'my beautiful husband.'"

"Did you indeed?" His gaze is warm.

I have pleased him, and I'm shocked at how much that knowledge pleases *me*.

"Go, little bird. Danelli will keep an eye on you. I will join you as soon as I can. I must speak with our host." He spears a look Martelli's way, but the man simply keeps on puffing.

I do as Rio says, but can't resist pausing at the door. I almost ask Martelli how his employee Antonio is doing to see if he'll react to the name, and to give Rio a heads-up about my suspicions.

I only just pull back before the query pops out. That information—and my instincts surrounding it—should be shared privately with Rio. Not used here simply as a possible jibe against an insufferable man.

Instead, I substitute a different rebuke. "Thank you for your hospitality, Mr. Martelli. You have a wonderful home, and I am sure your young daughter will be very happy with the elderly grandfather you have chosen for her to marry."

## 20

*"You don't stumble upon your heritage. It's there, just waiting to be explored and shared."*
Robbie Robertson

*Rio*

MY NAUGHTY WIFE needs a damn good spanking, and I will happily deliver one as soon as we are out of here. That last dig was far too much, but even so, I only just manage to hold back a hiss of laughter as she leaves.

Martelli almost chokes on his cigar when she delivers the taunt and flounces away before he can respond.

I have rarely loved Bianca more than in this very moment.

Martelli leans forward and smashes the cigar cherry so hard into the ashtray on the coffee table that the tray breaks in two with a loud crack. He curses in Italian and then swipes his hand in an angry gesture. The pump and refrigerated bag go flying. Seems we will not be bringing home any spare milk for Emilia.

I cross my arms and wait for his temper tantrum to subside, enjoying the lack of control he has just displayed. It is the subtle things that matter in a game of power, and Martelli has just put himself in the weaker position.

At least, for the moment.

He leaves the butt to burn itself out in the mess now strewn across the table. "You should be careful, Agosti. You are losing control—as is evidenced just now. That one will be the death of you if you are not careful, old friend."

I smile at him without humor. We are both aware who just lost control of his emotions, and it wasn't me.

"That *one*, as you call her, is my wife, and as such, she deserves respect. Even from you, Martelli. Just as I offer my respect when it comes to your wife."

I do not return the "friend" reference. We are not, and never have been, friends.

He inclines his head. "Agreed. Respect for our wives. Though it will only be a matter of time before you do stray from her bed. The likes of Julia Veneto, and others equally beautiful, are readily available at any time for men like us."

He's correct in regard to the availability of women. I wield great power in my position, as does Martelli himself. Power is a huge aphrodisiac. So too is money. And the fortunes we add to on a daily basis are immense.

My sexual appetites in the past are well known, and I have never been short of willing bed mates. But now that Bianca is in my life, I cannot imagine lusting after any other woman.

Even when she ran from me, before I found her and brought her home from Cleveland, I did not take another to

160

my bed. My obsession with her was the reason I swam thousands of laps in that damn pool above my club. Day after day. And the reason I barely slept until I had her back beneath my roof once again.

Whether physically in my life, or in my thoughts as a ghostly specter while she was gone, she filled every space in me until there was no room for anyone else.

There is no one else.

I know deep down that I have somehow met my match in Bianca. As unlikely as it seems, she has carved a place in my heart.

And now that she is back, I will never let her go.

---

*Bianca*

I DON'T WANT to leave Rio in there with Martelli. I don't trust that snake of a man, or his intentions toward my husband.

And I've likely just made the situation worse. I shouldn't have prodded our host with that stupid comment. If he took offence earlier, simply because I corrected him over my name, God knows what he'll do in regard to the jibe I just delivered about his daughter.

But he riled me so badly I couldn't help myself. I meant what I said, too. His daughter, who I've discovered tonight is a year younger than Angel. During the speeches, Martelli's future son-in-law was introduced, and I saw the expression on that poor girl's face when an old man who looked to be in his seventies stepped up to join her on the stage.

She is clearly not on board with marrying someone close to sixty years her senior.

161

I hope I haven't made things worse for Rio, by making my disgust for arranged marriages known.

It's pot and kettle, really, when I consider the circumstances of my own marriage. Not arranged, but forced. Far worse, when you consider it that way. At least Martelli's daughter will have time to get used to the idea. And perhaps, like Angel, she's always known her fate, and simply accepts it as the way things are done in this world.

I make a mental note to talk to Rio about Angel and try to ensure that whoever is "chosen" for her is at least a half-decent person.

Carlos Rossi is waiting when I return to the ballroom. He pounces as soon as I reenter through one of the arched openings. I just manage to hold back my sigh. The night has been interminably long, and I'm more than ready to head home with Rio.

*Home.*

I realize with a start that I am thinking of the Boston estate as home. Is that because I know Emilia is there, and wherever my daughter is, so too is my home? Or is my growing connection to that place something less tangible?

I don't have the chance to ponder. Rossi takes my elbow and leads me through another archway into an alcove slightly quieter than the raucous main area. Booze has been flowing all night, and the screams of laughter and conversations now are far louder than when Rio and I arrived.

"I wanted to take the opportunity to apologize properly to you, dear Bianca. We have not had the chance to speak much beyond our short exchange at the meeting in Boston."

There is reproach in his tone, and I detach from his grip. I study the lines and wrinkles of his face. I hadn't really noticed at the meeting, probably because I was too nervous that evening to notice anything much at all, but he looks a lot older than I remember, and it has only been a few months.

Is he waiting for Rio's hand to fall? For his time to be up the moment he is no longer seen as useful to my husband? I know firsthand how it feels to live in constant fear. It ages you far more quickly than nature intends.

"When you disappeared from Augusta and my men could not find you," he says, "you left me no choice. I had to come forward voluntarily and tell your husband at least something, or my whole family could have been wiped out of existence when he discovered my involvement."

I open my mouth to speak, but he holds up a hand. "I would not have come forward at all, if you had not disappeared. I would have protected you with my life. For your mother Rina's sake, Bianca."

My heart lurches. He really *did* love my mother.

"Will you tell me about my parents?" The request is impulsive; I want to know more, of course, but I've avoided asking. Maybe because I'm afraid of the answers.

But I know so little, and now that I have Emilia, I want to find out more so I can help her understand her true heritage when she's old enough.

Rossi hesitates, then moves across to a wrought-iron bench positioned at one side of the alcove. When he takes a seat and pats the bench beside him, I cross and perch on the edge.

"You know I was in love with your mother," he begins, and I nod.

"Yes, that was obvious from the first time we met."

He laughs lightly, but there is little humor in the sound. "I could never act on that love because Rina was besotted with your father. And Stefano, my dear, was very much like Rio is now. The Boss of the Carlotti family, and utterly ruthless if anyone dared to cross him."

"But my mother…loved him anyway?"

"With all her heart and soul," Rossi says softly. "She and Stefano were betrothed from a young age in a marriage arranged by their families." There's a faint hint of bitterness underlying his words when he adds, "You will not like to hear this, but it is fortunate they died together in that bomb blast. She would have been only half a person without her Stefano in this world. No one would ever have been able to fill her heart the way he did."

Not even her daughter? I swallow down the sudden lump in my throat, wondering if I could ever be as heartless if it came to Emilia. Of course, my mother likely had no choice about whether she lived or died in that moment, but if she *had* survived, would I ever have been enough for her?

My eyes smart, and I blink hard, refusing to cry over a woman I never knew. My parents were the loving couple who raised me. If I have to cry at some point, then let it be over the fact that my adoptive mother never had the chance to meet her granddaughter, and my adoptive father was so heartbroken over her death that he disappeared into the mountains somewhere in Thailand and doesn't even know he has a grandchild.

"So, my birth father had plenty of enemies, then?"

Like Rio.

"Indeed, he did. There were even some within the Carlotti family itself. *Your* family, Bianca. A jostling behind closed doors for control of the organization. It is not known to this day who ordered the hit, but the belief is that someone didn't like the direction in which your father was trying to take the business."

"What direction was that?" I feel strangely disconnected, as if we're discussing characters from a book or movie.

But the reality is they were my family. My *parents*. My own flesh and blood.

"I was not privy to the details, but there was talk around the time that he was considering selling off portions of the business to other families. He wanted to raise capital to invest in new ventures, but some saw the strategy as one that would weaken the Carlotti power base. Our host this evening, Gianni Martelli, was one of those purported to be an interested party."

My fingers, already clenched in my lap, convulse slightly at that revelation. Martelli seems far less stable than the man sitting in front of me, and he would make a frightening enemy. Though I have to remember that Rossi's grandfather-like persona is just a front. I've seen glimpses of the hardness beneath several times, and I'm sure he would be a formidable foe, too.

"And you, Carlos?" I ask. "Were you an interested party?"

"Perhaps, but it is all a long time ago now, my dear. And all moot. Your husband has control of the Carlotti empire, thanks to your marriage, and I am the last person he would ever consider conducting business with these days."

"Is that because of me? Because you helped me?"

"Ah. It is for many reasons. And I am under no illusions. You and I both know I am likely on borrowed time when it comes to Rio's plans for me. But I have provided information to Rio, and he believes I have more to offer. For that reason and that alone, I am not currently six feet under."

I flinch at the directness of his statement, but he's likely telling the truth. There have been too many transgressions involving Carlos Rossi, even though he never seems to be at fault. Rio is unlikely to allow Carlos to live unless he sees a benefit for the Agostis.

"I owe you an apology, too, Carlos," I admit. "I took your money under false pretenses. I have to admit that I had no intention of stopping at the apartment you arranged for me in Augusta. And for that, I'm sorry."

"You did not wish to swap one crime lord for another, hmm?"

"Well... I..."

Luckily, I manage to suppress my shudder because he laughs as if he can perceive my discomfort and enjoys it.

"As your benefactor, my dear. Nothing more."

"Oh." My cheeks heat, and I briefly drop my gaze to my feet. "That assessment is kind of accurate," I admit after a moment. "I just needed to get as far away from this some-times-violent world as I could. After what happened with Anders."

"Ah. And because he was my man, you blamed me?"

"No. I believed you when you said you had no knowledge of that attack. And I made sure to get that information to Rio as you asked."

"Yes, you did, and I am grateful. *That* is one of the reasons I am alive right now."

I swallow hard, hoping he doesn't take offence at my next words. "It's just that you are part of that world. You and Rio both, Carlos. And I was afraid for my baby. I just had to get away. I'm sorry, but it's true."

His eyes soften. "You speak the truth, my dear. This *is* often a violent world. Unfortunately, the moment Rio kidnapped and then married you, you became part of it. And no matter how fast or how far you run, you will never escape it. Not anymore. Especially not now that you have brought his child into the world."

I know how accurate that observation is. I've been going over that very fact in my head and seeing it play out in my own actions even before I could articulate it in a conscious manner. I am now locked in this life, and I don't see how I can ever get out. Alive.

I jump to my feet, stumble over to one of the grand columns that marks the entrance to this alcove, and lean my back against the cool marble. I need to concentrate on breathing, slow and steady, to try and tamp down the underlying panic that threatens my surface calm.

The moment Emilia was born, something irrevocably changed.

Even if one day Rio and I decide to end our marriage, he will always be in my life as Emilia's dad. Not an average soccer-on-weekends kind of dad, but still a father nonetheless.

I can never escape, no matter how much I may want to. The only way I can see to protect myself and my child from now on is to fully trust the one man I ran from.

Rio himself.

## 21

*"We live in a fantasy world, a world of illusion. The great
task in life is to find reality."*
Iris Murdoch

*Rio*

MY CONCERN RISES after the conversation with Martelli. He
finally admitted to experiencing several similar business
upheavals to the ones we're having in Boston. I'm still not
convinced it is not his outfit causing the issues.

But there was a look in his eyes—a genuine apprehension
—that spoke of truth. Someone is out to upset the natural
order and balance of our world.

So, when I reenter the ballroom and can't see Bianca
anywhere, my concern skyrockets and my breathing
shortens.

Where is she? Has she run again? Is she safe?

I should not have brought her with me on this trip. What was I thinking?

Truth is, I wasn't thinking. Not with my head, anyway. I never do when it comes to Bianca.

I pull my cell from my jacket pocket and am about to dial Danelli—to hell with Martelli's fucking rule about no security except his own—when I spy my wife emerging from behind a column. She looks…shaken, for want of a better word.

Moments later, Rossi appears beside her. He pats her arm and then leaves her there alone. I barrel across the room. She looks up and sees me coming, flinching when I grab her elbow.

"What is it? Did he hurt you?"

She blinks a couple of times, possibly at the venom in my tone, and the distressed expression fades. She shoots me a crooked smile. "No, all good. He apologized, I apologized… All good."

Clearly, she's not okay. I'm done with this charade of an event. We need to get out of here.

"Time to leave, Bianca," I announce, and keep my hand firmly on her elbow as I steer her toward the exit.

"Thank God," she murmurs, and while we wait at the building entrance for a staff member to call for the car that will deliver us to the airport, she turns to face me and gives me a genuine smile this time. "I've been ready to leave since the moment we arrived. I can't wait to get home."

Warmth blooms in my chest, replacing the concern that had held my muscles tight. *Home*? "I like the sound of that word on your lips, little bird."

"Which one?" she teases. "Leave?"

"You know which one."

Whatever upset her in her conversation with Rossi, she seems to have thrown it off quickly. I will find out what they discussed, but not right now.

Something changed between us when Emilia was born. Whatever it is is indefinable in my mind, but it is the reason I allowed her to accompany me here tonight. It is the reason a fierce protectiveness has arisen deep inside me. It is the reason I now begin to understand the true power—and danger—of love, when it has never touched my heart in the past.

And the indefinable *thing* between us is the reason I study her delicate features and her voluptuous curves right now, and imagine all the things I will do to her even before we reach the Boston estate.

*Home.*

"I am going to make you scream tonight, Bianca. In the skies far above this crowd of sycophantic hangers-on. When the jet takes off, so will you. I will be relentless, and you will be begging for more before we are even halfway home."

Her wide mouth parts, and the tip of her tongue darts out to moisten her bottom lip. Those are the lips that I will soon order to be wrapped around my cock. Desire floods through me at the mental image, and my trousers begin to tent.

I am no teenage boy, and I can control my body if I wish. But I do not wish. I want her to know how much I desire her, to drown in the scent of my arousal. I want her to imagine the hot taste of my need on that sexy little tongue as her pussy lips dampen with her own slick excitement.

"That's a big promise, husband," she murmurs, her eyes shuttering briefly as she flutters her lashes. "It's a short plane ride."

"It is long enough, Bianca, for foreplay. A beginning. And

then we will continue the rest long into the night after we arrive back in Boston. To our home."

The shiver that runs through her is visible even in the darkness of the night around us, and I smile, enjoying the knowledge of what that shiver means. It may be edged with something less positive than desire—in fact, it almost certainly is, knowing the complex nature of our relationship —but even if she still fears me, or loathes this life into which she has been thrust, she cannot hide her need. Not from me. The scent of it rises around us, increasing as the car glides to a stop beneath the portico at the entrance, and I hand her into the rear compartment of the limo.

My fingers graze her hip as I steady her, the little hitch of her breath confirming her super-aware state. I told her once that desire is a two-edged sword. Fear and need. Love and hate. Enemies and passionate lovers.

I am about to deliver on all fronts. My wife will never be the same again.

———

*Bianca*

*I AM GOING to make you scream tonight.*

He has promised that in the past, and always managed to deliver, even when I was determined not to let it happen. Will tonight be any different? Will I be able to maintain any control of my body? Over my emotions? Over my own damn voice?

Do I *want* to maintain control?

The truth is, I want my husband to make me scream. And

when I look into the darkness of his eyes, I know I've already lost this battle.

The jet takes off, and once we're airborne and the captain provides permission to move around the cabin, Rio orders all staff out of the main lounge area.

He tells them to return only in the event of an emergency, and for anything less, there will be consequences. Everyone scurries away, and finally it is just myself and Rio in the compact space. We sit in cream leather lounge seats, facing each other in silence.

I am almost vibrating with need, my core wet and ready, and he has not laid a single finger on me since he helped me into the limo at Martelli's estate.

"What do you want, Rio?" My voice is breathier than I would like.

But his eyes tell me he already knows, even without hearing the need in my tone, how much I want him.

"What do I want?" he begins in a conversational tone, but then the heat simmering between us both seems to flare, and he finishes in a far rougher voice. "I want you to kneel for me, my wife. Right here, right now. Come here. *Faster*."

I jump up from my seat and take a step forward, then slowly lower to the floor of the cabin in front of him and shuffle forward on my knees. His legs drift wider, making a space for me between his thighs, and the material of his suit trousers pulls across his swollen flesh.

"Release me."

I wet my lips, the ache in my body growing. I reach out to undo his button and the zipper, allowing his cock to pop free in all its erect glory. My core is slick, my pussy lips heavy, and I can't help the moan that slips out.

"Now touch me, Bianca. Stroke me, and then bend your

head and take me in your mouth. And when you do so, you may imagine my mouth devouring *you*. Licking at your clit, drinking in your juices, and then invading your wet channel with my tongue and my exploring fingers."

I grip his hard flesh and slide my hand up and down, running my thumb over the tip and spreading the drop of pre-cum waiting for me. He leans back in his seat, resting the back of his head against the leather, looking up at the ceiling of the cabin as if he's bored with my touch. But I note the bob of his Adam's apple as he swallows, and the rapid rise and fall of his chest as his breathing quickens.

I tighten my fist, slide faster, and there it is. A tiny groan that he cannot control.

I am smiling in triumph as I lean in and take his cock into my mouth. I love the knowledge that I can arouse him so easily. That a man so powerful and in control in the rest of his life can be brought undone by the lick and swirl of my lips and tongue and teeth.

I love the taste of him, the scent of him. The feel of his silken flesh so hard and hot within my mouth and throat. But I love more than anything his shudders as he begins to buck and thrust beneath me.

In pleasuring him, my own need ramps up to unbearable levels, and I moan around his flesh, wanting him deep inside me.

As if he can sense my frustration, he pushes me off him and drags me up onto his lap in one quick move. He takes my mouth with a kiss so deep it is almost punishing in its intensity.

My dress shucks up over my hips, and his fingers knead my ass before his grip tightens and constricts, then the sound of ripping fabric fills the cabin. I break off the kiss and look down at his left hand, which now holds my panties. Torn in two. Again.

I'm going to have to get in a whole new supply of underwear, just for Rio.

He throws them aside and begins to kiss me again, and I grind my now-bare pussy against his organ. I'm desperate for release and try to rise up and impale myself on him. But he won't let me. He holds my hips in place, preventing me from doing so. Instead, I rub frantically against him, my moans turning almost feral.

His lips leave mine and trail down my neck, and his fingers, previously rough and greedy, turn featherlight as he grazes the sides of my aching breasts.

"Fuck me, Rio, please. *Please!*"

"Not yet, my beautiful little bird. I haven't made you scream."

He shifts position in the chair, somehow sliding out from beneath me and flipping us so that I'm seated and he is now kneeling on the floor in front of me. The leather on my bare ass is warm from his body heat. Even that creates a flame to my need.

He grins, a wolfish expression that inspires yet another ache to ripple right through me and center in my core. He drags a finger languidly through my wetness and brings it to his lips.

"Your essence is like nectar, Bianca. I want all of it. But not yet. You may not come, wife, until I have drunk my fill. Do you understand me?"

Holy hell. How am I going to hold on? I'm ready to climax right now, especially when he parts my legs and looks down at my exposed pussy with that dark and enticing expression.

And then he leans in and claims me with his mouth, and I almost shatter on the spot.

But I can't. Not without his permission...

It is my turn to buck and shudder beneath his ministrations as he gives me back as good as I gave. His tongue laps at my entrance, darts inside, and then returns to circle and tease my clit while one, then two, of his fingers slips inside my wetness.

I sound like an animal, moaning and groaning and growling, but I don't care. I have to wait like he said. I have to hold off from coming...but it's so hard; it's too hard. He's so fucking good at eating me out and fucking me with his fingers that I can't bear to hold on a moment longer... I have to...

"Come now, baby," he commands against my hot, wet flesh. "Come for me. Right. *Now*."

He sucks on my clit and spears me with his fingers one more time, and I break apart beneath him.

The scream tears out of me as I come, and then even as I'm shuddering and pulsing from the force of the climax, he lifts me off the chair and rolls back to lie on the carpeted floor of the cabin with me straddling him. This time he lets me sink down onto his ready cock, and I begin to ride in a frenzy.

The tension in my body, only just released, instantly ramps into overdrive as he thrusts upward to meet my rocking motion. I can't hold on. The torture is too exquisite, and I begin to come again, this time my channel walls squeezing around his organ as I let loose another scream.

He roars too, and we fall together over the cliff edge of sensation into the most mind-blowing orgasm of my life.

It is only after, when I come to my senses still lying atop him, our hearts beating fast in tandem, that I begin to sob. He has taken every little part of me—from my name to my body to my very sense of identity—and reformed me into someone I barely recognize.

And now I know that no matter what he does, no matter what he *is*, I can never be whole again without him—my monster—in my life.

---

*"To be trusted is a greater compliment than being loved."*
George McDonald

*Bianca*

THERE IS no actual discussion about it, but when we arrive at the estate, Rio orders my things moved from my bedroom next door, into his suite. The final step in bringing us together. The decision itself, as well as my lack of annoyance about the non-consultation, signals some kind of turning point in our relationship with one another. Yet another turning point, only this is one I never thought I would reach.

I'm still in love with my husband, as I have been for so long.

But I don't think I hate him anymore.

We fall into a pattern that involves Rio disappearing during the day to work in the city and returning to the estate

—and to our bed—at night. I can almost convince myself that we are living a normal and comfortable married life.

Almost.

If it weren't for the increased security around the estate and the growing tension I sense within Rio every time he arrives home. He's obviously still concerned about whatever upheaval is going on in his business, but he's trying not to let me see it.

Despite the underlying tension, he is giving me more freedom these days than he did before the Washington trip. That may be partly because Angelica is in residence and clearly not happy to hang out at home, and she is not shy about making her wishes known. She wants me to accompany her on her various outings, and won't take no for an answer.

If I'd had a younger sister, I would have loved her to turn out just like Angel. Sweet and kind-natured, but with a hidden fire in her belly that doesn't put up with any nonsense.

I suspect Rio is going to have his work cut out for him if he tries to choose her a husband as elderly as Gianni Martelli's new son-in-law-to-be.

The day Emilia turns six months old, Angel convinces her brother to let us have a trip into the city. Not to visit him at the club, but to pretend we're tourists and do the Freedom Trail, with the plan being to grab lunch at a café along the way.

It sounds so "normal" that tears unexpectedly burn my eyes when Angel confirms that Rio has given permission.

"Along with about five thousand rules we need to follow, of course. And we'll have an entourage of security. But we can take Emilia, too, if you like. And Penn. And maybe afterward Penn can take Emilia home, and we can go to a bar or something and have a bit of fun."

I slant her a sideways look. "Ah, hon, you're under twenty-one, remember? And your family *owns* a bar. Several bars and clubs, as far as I can gather. Not that I'd take you anyway, but at which bar or club do you think you'd be able to get away with underage drinking?"

"Spoilsport." She pouts, then brightens. "Well, I'll be twenty soon, so I won't have to wait too much longer. Okay, let's do it minus the bar part, then."

Her enthusiasm is so contagious I find myself full of anticipation when our "entourage," as Angel puts it, makes our way into the city. I gave Penn the day off in the end, so it's just Angel, Emilia, and me, together with Lee, who seems to draw wife-watching duty more than most of the team, plus three other goons whose names I'm not familiar with.

A fifth team member drops us off at Boston Common and advises he'll drive ahead so we can reach him easily along the way if we need to. Lee steps up to help me unfold the stroller and load Emilia in. She's strong for her age and has just started sitting up, so I know she'll enjoy being able to look out and about as we walk.

It's cold today, so we're all bundled up. But at least it isn't raining. I'm ridiculously excited. Having lived in Boston for much of my life with my adoptive parents, it's crazy that I've never walked the Trail. Neither has Angel, apparently, so we're both as green as any tourist when we start in the direction of the State House.

"Did you know this is America's first public park?" Lee's voice murmurs from behind us, and both Angel and I turn to face him.

He shoots us an embarrassed grin, as if he didn't mean to reveal any of his non-goon humanity.

I grin back, not letting him off the hook. "No, I didn't

know that. What other little tidbits of information are you hiding in that brain of yours, Lee?"

"Not much," he mutters, and we keep walking. "It was established in 1634," he adds after a minute.

Angel and I exchange a look, and then share a laugh. Lee is definitely growing on me.

I shove away the recalcitrant thought that whispers, *Let's hope he doesn't die like Leon did.*

We're having the best day, approaching the Old Corner Bookstore and talking about where we might stop to eat, when a blonde-haired woman steps out of the shadows of a building doorway and approaches our little group.

She's wearing jeans, a shirt, and low-heeled boots that are slightly scuffed. Her long overcoat is unbuttoned, showing cuffs hanging from her belt, and from the bulge under the coat, she's clearly carrying a weapon.

"Oh my God." I come to an abrupt stop, clutching the stroller and my heart rate ratcheting up.

A sense of déjà vu hits me, only this time, unlike outside the animal rescue center, I have Emilia to worry about.

Then my brain clicks into gear, focusing on more than just the presence of the gun, and I recognize her.

*Felicity.* If that's her real name.

The goons sense danger and swing into action, surrounding us as one with their hands heading for their weapons.

"Wait, wait, *please.*" I direct my plea at Lee, who seems to be the one in charge today. "I know her. She's a cop. Well, a Fed. I think. Don't draw your weapons, *please.* I don't want anyone to get into trouble."

Or die.

Angel steps in closer to me as if to draw comfort. Or to

protect me. Who knows? Given she's an Agosti, it could be either option.

Felicity smiles, but it doesn't reach her eyes. "How are you today, Mrs. Agosti? I trust all these gentlemen have firearms licenses?"

I meet her gaze squarely, even though my breathing is still shorter than usual. "They do. We can waste everyone's time checking, if you wish, but we both know Rio would never send out his men without the correct paperwork in place."

I have no idea if that's true or not, but I trust Rio's arrangements. At this point, I have to.

It seems she does, too, because she takes another step closer to me without reaching for her gun. I resist the urge to jump in front of the stroller and hide Emilia from her sharp gaze, and instead, watch her approach.

When the goons go to stop her, I wave a hand. "It's okay, guys. She obviously wants to talk, and she's not going to hurt me. Or arrest me."

I hope.

At the very least, though, she's probably fuming about my disappearing act last year. She and her colleagues thought I would turn on my husband and give them the information they needed to finally arrest Rio and put him away. And at one point, I might have actually done it. But so much has changed since then. She must have been sorely disappointed, and possibly embarrassed on a professional level too if she'd sold my betrayal to her superiors and then I disappeared straight afterward.

Her eyes narrow, and this time when she moves forward, there's a new wariness in her features. "I do wish to talk," she confirms. "Can we have a few minutes, Bree?" She seems to realize her error and quickly corrects herself. "Sorry. Bianca. Mrs. Agosti. Can we talk…alone?"

"No. We can't." I link my left arm through Angel's to show I mean it, and grip the stroller handle hard with my other hand. "We can talk for a minute, if you want, Felicity, but not alone. You can say whatever you need to in front of the others."

"Right, then." She puts her hands on her hips, studying me first before looking down at Emilia and back again. "Congratulations on the birth. I heard he grabbed you back and forced you to stay here till you'd had his baby."

"It wasn't quite like that." *It was*, a little voice whispers at the back of my mind. *It was exactly like that.*

"Wasn't it? Come on, Bianca, get real. The man's a criminal. Do you really want your child brought up in that lifestyle? Isn't that why you tried to get away last time? What happened? Did he threaten you?"

Angel bristles at my side. "You're talking about my brother, lady. The head of our family. Watch how you speak about Rio."

I shake her arm a little. "Leave it, Angel. Please. Don't make unnecessary waves for yourself." Then I turn back to the federal agent. "He didn't threaten me, Felicity. He didn't know I was planning to leave. If you want to blame someone for that, it's all on me. Not him."

Felicity ignores Angel and keeps her gaze on me. Her expression turns pitying. "We can help you, Bianca. Our door is still open. You just need to reach out, and we'll be there."

The thing is, I don't believe Felicity is my enemy. She may be an enemy of my husband's, being on the opposite side of the law to him, but she isn't trying to make things hard for me. Or trick me into anything I don't want to do. She may have been happy to use me to get to Rio last time, and I'm sure she still is, but there's no doubt she sees it as a win-win for both of us.

The anger that started to rise in me when I first saw her fades at the realization that she's probably still genuinely trying to reach out and help me.

And deep down, I know that everything she says is true. Rio *is* a criminal, and I *don't* want my daughter brought up in this crazy, violent life. But this time round, things are different. I'm not the person I was. I've changed. And even if I wanted to—which I don't—I will never go back to being the person I was before Rio first snatched me off the street.

Bree Walker is dead. I am Bianca Carlotti-Agosti, and it is time everyone—including me—accepts that.

"No, Felicity." I keep my tone gentle but firm. "I'm not who I was last year. I'm Rio Agosti's wife now. The mother of his child. And I love him. I will not betray him again. Don't wait for me to reach out because you'll be waiting forever."

I look at Angel, and then at Lee. "Come on, guys. Shall we finish the Trail?"

I push the stroller and walk on past Felicity, who stands there with her fists clenching and unclenching. I keep my chin up and my manner calm, even though I'm scared she'll suddenly lash out and grab me. She has those cuffs hanging off her belt and a whole lot of frustration simmering in that body of hers, I'm sure.

But then our group is past her, and I begin to breathe more naturally. That is, until her annoyed voice rings out after us.

"He got to you, Bree. I know it. And now you've chosen a

side. The *wrong* side. Good luck trying to raise your kid safely to adulthood."

She seriously went *there*? I swing back, ready to fling a barb straight back at her, but she's already disappeared into the shadows. I settle for an inarticulate growl of frustration.

Angel leans down, grabs one of the baby wipes under the stroller, and then hands it to me.

"What…"

"Your face. You're sweating a bit."

"Oh. Thanks." I hadn't realized a sheen of sweat had broken out on my brow.

*Thanks, Felicity, for nothing*, I think, swiping at my brow.

"Well, that was totally awks," Angel says when I'm done, and I force out a laugh in response.

"It was a bit. And let me tell you, Angel, if you *were* twenty-one, we would definitely be calling Penn back to her duty and handing off Emilia. I could do with a drink. I haven't had one since I found out I was pregnant, but I could sure use one thanks to that damn woman."

The rest of our outing is uneventful, but the initial joy in the excursion has fizzled out, for all of us, I think, based on the glum faces of the team, and we only make it as far as the Paul Revere House before Angel and I decide we've finally had enough, and Lee calls in the car to pick us up and head home.

I wonder which one of them will make it to Rio first to tell him about today's run-in. My money is on Lee.

During the ride home, I have time to wonder what Rio's response will be, and whether he'll fling me straight back down into the dungeon and we'll have to start rebuilding trust all over again.

I meant what I said to the agent. I'm determined not to

184

betray my husband again, at least not knowingly. But in this world of deceit, fear, and violence, I can never fully promise anything because the playing field is never level, and it tilts and bucks on a daily basis.

I stroke Emilia's soft dark hair as she sits placidly beside me in her car seat. She has fallen asleep, as she often does in the car, her dark lashes caressing her pink cheeks with the simple beauty of an innocent child. She is my only true constant. And I know, deep down, that if my daughter is ever under direct threat, by anyone, all bets will be off.

## 23

*"The argument of danger only applies to those who live in relative safety."*
Graham Greene

*Rio*

IT IS BARELY DUSK when I return home from the club. The sun is lowering toward the horizon, and shadows lengthen over the estate as my car navigates the long driveway to the entrance of the main building.

One wouldn't know, looking out on the landscaped gardens surrounding the building, and the neat expanse of grass that slopes away down toward the river, that there is a network of rooms beneath the estate. My father had them built as a safety net many years ago, but they hadn't been brought into play until the attack by Anders's men.

My sister greets me at the front door and accompanies

me down to my underground office, walking jauntily beside me and clearly wanting to share something important.

She waits until I pour a whiskey from the side table and then sit behind my desk before she perches on the edge of the visitor's chaise. She then proceeds to explain what happened during her outing with Bianca today.

My first instinct on hearing that agent's name is to pull out my gun from its holstered place beneath my desk and shoot something.

How dare the Feds try a second time to entice my wife to betray me?

The need for violent action is almost overwhelming, but I manage to contain my rage and breathe calmly while my sister continues to talk. She seems unaware of how close I've just come to losing control, and for that, I'm grateful. She has been away at boarding school for much of her life, and as such has been sheltered from a lot of the violence that permeates our world.

But if Bianca ever says yes once again to helping the Feds, I will not be responsible for my actions. No matter who is sitting there watching me.

*But she hasn't*, I remind myself over and over. Angel has just confirmed that my wife sent the agent on her way. Bianca didn't say yes. She said no.

As soon as Angel leaves, I call in Danelli. He has been following up the various Antonios we had identified as possible saboteurs, and I need to know what he's found out. There was another attack on one of our warehouses earlier today, and if I don't regain the upper hand soon, I may as well put a bullet in my own head. Or hand the gun to my nearest rival and stand mute while they finish me off. The whole situation is out of control, and my reputation is hanging by a thread.

I'm beginning to wonder if we've been given the wrong information. What if Rossi is playing us all? What if he's planted the notion of an Antonio, and it is someone else altogether? My skin is buzzing with the knowledge that something is off. I just can't pinpoint what it is.

But first, I need to confirm my sister's story. Angelica is still young and always believes the best of people. I need a more experienced viewpoint.

"You have spoken with the team who accompanied my wife on her outing today?"

"I had the Alpha team on them today. And yes, I have spoken with Leon." His face remains calm, which begins to quiet my own inner beast. Clearly, there is nothing alarming to report. "I have requested Leon put the details into an email report for you, but there is nothing to be concerned about. The woman, Felicity, wanted to talk alone with your wife, but Bianca wouldn't allow it. And from Leon's summary, your wife made it crystal clear that the Feds won't get any cooperation from her moving forward."

"Good." The *thing* deep inside me—the darkness that always threatens to rise when it senses danger—relaxes back into a state of watchfulness.

Bianca did well today. She will no doubt call me out for being patronizing when I tell her later, but I am proud of the woman she has become.

I lift my whiskey and take a sip, enjoying the smoky flavor for a moment before I change the subject. "Now. Antonio. The one at the wharf, and any others you've managed to find. What of them?"

"A dead end, Boss," he confirms.

He still stands at attention in front of my desk. I invite him to sit and offer him a drink, but as usual, he refuses. He likes to maintain a certain formality between us. He's an excellent second, so I indulge him in his need for little formalities. As well as his slightly cringeworthy love of all things military.

"They are all dead ends so far," he adds drily. "I've never had so much difficulty tracking down an individual. Are you sure..."

He swallows back whatever else he was about to say.

I lower my eyebrows and stare at him. "Speak your mind. You are my second. You are allowed to question my judgment—though only in private. What is it, Danelli?"

"I just wonder if we're chasing a ghost, Boss. Someone who doesn't exist." He runs an agitated hand through his hair.

It isn't often that my second shows his frustration so clearly.

I share both his frustration and his views on this matter. "I have been thinking the same," I confirm. "The name Antonio came from one source in the first instance. It is easy to start rumors once an initial story is out there, is it not?"

His lips thin, and he nods slightly. "That source being...Rossi."

"Indeed. We always come back to him. I want the man kept alive a little longer. Because I want to dig deeper into the circumstances surrounding my parents' deaths, as well as those of my wife's parents. My instincts are telling me Rossi knows more than he has let on. I think it is time to change tack on our saboteur investigation, Danelli. Look into Rossi instead. See what you can find. And do it fast. My gut is screaming at me that we're running out of time. Whatever is brewing will soon come to a head. I am certain of it."

He rubs his arms, as if my words have made him cold. "I think so too, Boss. I'm on it."

When he leaves, I steeple my fingers and stare at the drink on the desk in front of me, considering pieces of the puzzle. Pieces that make no sense. Not yet, anyway. Danger is on the horizon. It is circling our family, and I have not been able to identify the source.

Only one piece seems to sit right in the center of the puzzle every time. Carlos Rossi.

It is time he and I had another talk. A talk on my terms, not his.

But first, there is something I need to do—something I should have done months ago. I pick up my cell and dial my lawyer. He answers instantly—I pay him enough on retainer that he knows never to keep me waiting.

"I need you to draw up some papers, Carnarvon. Have them ready by tomorrow evening, and meet me in my office above the club."

---

### Bianca

RIO IS UNUSUALLY quiet at dinner. He is naturally taciturn, rare to smile or laugh, but even for him, it is noticeable that his thoughts are elsewhere. At first, I wonder if it may be because of my inadvertent meeting with Felicity, which I'm sure his team told him about. But he grunts and shakes his head when I ask.

"I am not concerned about that, Bianca. On the contrary, I am very proud of you," he says. "You did well today, by all reports. You showed your loyalty to our family."

I pout at him, mock-annoyed. "That's a little condescending, Rio. Do I deserve a little pat on the head, too?"

I would never have had the nerve to say such a thing to him even a month or two ago, but there's a growing ease between us that emboldens me sometimes.

Especially when he's pensive, like he is now. I want to snap him out of it, ease whatever worries are keeping him mentally locked away from me. It seems I've succeeded when he releases a small huff of laughter.

"I told Danelli you would call me out for my patronizing attitude. You proved me right."

His mouth is still lifted at the corners in a show of good humor, and I laugh, too.

"Thank you, Rio. I'm glad I could be of service."

"Oh, I can think of a much more interesting way you can be of service, little bird."

The sensual words roll over me, and I am about to jump up from my seat at the table and sashay around to wriggle onto his lap, but I pause in the act of rising. There was something hollow in his tone that doesn't ring true.

So, instead of responding to his teasing comment in that way, I lower back into my chair and frown at him. "Is everything all right, Rio? Are you all right? Are...*we*?"

"We are fine, Bianca. I just have several things on my mind at present. Which reminds me... I will have Danelli's men bring you in to the club tomorrow evening. I have some papers to go through with you regarding Emilia's future. We need to ensure her financial security so that if anything were to happen to either of us, she will be well looked after."

"I... Well, okay. That sounds...sensible." It doesn't sound sensible. It sounds terrifying.

Both the thought that Rio and I may be about to die, and

the fact that he's going to make me go back to that club. The place where I witnessed so much death.

But I don't get the chance to ask if we can go through the paperwork here instead, as Rio is already speaking again.

"Carnarvon will bring the papers upstairs at six, and once we've signed everything, I will take you out for dinner afterward. With Angel and Nicky."

"Oh, that'll be…nice." My heart sinks.

I'm not particularly raring to see Nicky again anytime soon. But Rio continues, oblivious to my trepidation.

"Angel will already be in the city—she told me she's spending the afternoon with our brother so we can all meet up afterward. It will be good to spend more time as a family."

I smile at him, but my earlier thoughts about writhing on his lap and being thoroughly seduced by him have now dissipated into nothing. Lost in the dust of reality.

And when we finally head to bed, he does not try to make love with me as he usually does, either. Instead, he simply pulls me close and wraps me in his strong embrace. I rest my head on his chest, the vibration of his heart beating steadily against my cheek, in a moment that calms my jangled nerves and stretches out into several minutes.

This feels far more intimate than any sexual act.

"I love you, Rio," I murmur into the silence, not wanting this moment to end.

After a minute, his breath tickles my hair, and his lips graze the top of my head. "You and Emilia are my everything, Bianca. Whatever happens in the future, I wish you to know that, *mia cara*."

"I do know that," I answer, and his arms tighten around me.

But the moment of intimacy is broken as thoughts of danger and threats begin to crowd back into my mind.

*Whatever happens in the future...* In this world, there is violence lurking around every corner.

And for some reason, it feels as if that violence is coming closer every day.

## 24

*"Things are seldom what they seem."*
W.S. Gilbert

*Rio*

I DECIDE to meet Carnarvon and my wife in the club itself rather than my office above because Bianca hasn't been back here since the shootout, and I want to prove to her there is nothing for her to fear here anymore.

I've noticed she avoids certain places at the estate—those specific spots where she knows people were killed—but she doesn't have the same avoidance issue there as she does with this place. It doesn't take rocket science to understand that's because she was here when it all went down, and so the club is far more tied to her trauma memories than anywhere else.

My team worked hard—and quickly—to remove all traces of the violence and destruction. The couches in the VIP area are new since then, as are the carpets and fittings. The modern-luxe look is similar to what was in place before, but there is no evidence to link back to blood, bullet casings, or traces of body matter.

No matter how hard the police tried to find some. And try damn hard, they did.

It took a few weeks for the crowds to return, but the location is good, and the club's reputation is significant in this city. We are now busier than ever. Right now, being only just past six p.m., it is far too early for the crowds that will fill the space later in the night. But the bar is open, and there are many patrons from nearby offices already drinking and laughing as they wind down after their day at work.

I expect Bianca to be wary, coming back here. I stand on the raised dais area, leaning my back against the glass-paneled railing and watching the elevator bank closely so I can greet her as soon as she arrives and try to allay any concern she may have.

When the silver doors glide open, Bianca steps out, followed closely by Leon—the man she calls Lee—and the other regular on her detail, Mitch. She stops, her gaze darting around, and I see her swallow before her arms wrap across her middle. It is her usual tell. She only does that when she feels particularly unsettled.

She has dressed up for the visit in a cream-colored minidress that hugs her curves as she moves. Her hair is down, tumbling past her shoulders just as I like it, and the familiar thread of desire hums through me.

So many men in our world have a wife at home and a mistress—or several mistresses—on the side. I have no need of a mistress. My wife satisfies my every sexual craving, and I cannot imagine a time when she won't.

The two men with her scan the room, noting my men already in place, and both turn to give me a respectful nod as I start toward them.

Before I can reach her, a business-suited man at the bar slides off his stool and heads toward the elevators. Leon stiffens, but then relaxes when the man appears to have no interest in Bianca. He is simply a patron who has finished his drink and obviously wants to head home.

Bianca gives the man a polite smile, then turns and pushes the button to keep the elevator in place for him.

As she turns back to face me, the man bumps her slightly. She looks startled, not hurt, and then the man utters what seems to be some kind of quiet apology before he pushes a small envelope into her hand.

It all happens in the space of a second or two, and he disappears into the waiting elevator car. The doors slide closed before I fully process what I've just seen.

She's fine. Everything is fine. Then why is my gut suddenly roiling with tension?

And why is she standing frozen with that stricken look on her face?

Leon is staring at the closed elevator doors.

"Stop him!" I yell, and Leon jumps toward the elevator, banging on the button.

Too late. The car must already be on the way down. He speaks urgently into his mic, and I presume he's contacting someone on the first floor to stop the guy when he gets down there.

Bianca finally moves, coming out of her previously frozen state and shaking her head. She glances down at the envelope in her hand and frowns, as if she isn't even certain how she got it.

What the fuck did that man say to her?

Mitch puts out a hand to take the envelope from her, but she turns away from him and starts to open it.

Alarm bells chime in my head, and I launch the final couple of steps toward her. No idea what's in the envelope, but it won't be good.

I'm too late. She pulls out a handful of photographs. Her eyes widen, and she drops them to the floor where they scatter around her gold-colored heels.

She falls to her knees and starts to gather up the photos in frenetic haste, along with a typewritten note tucked in amongst them. When I look down to see what they are, my heart skips a beat before shock infuses every cell in my body.

---

### Bianca

MY DAUGHTER'S innocent smiling face stares back up at me from the floor, in photos clearly taken yesterday on the Trail walk. There are photos of me, too, and Angel, but I zero in on Emilia. They were there, watching us, and we didn't know.

How could we not know? How could *I* not sense someone getting close enough to take photos of my child?

There's far more fuelling my shock than these photos, but I can't process the rest right now. It's too much. Too obscenely unbelievable.

No. Don't think about what the man said. He was lying. He had to be. Think about the rest later.

*Focus on these photos*, my brain instructs. *And the note that comes with them.*

The note that says: *It is time for you to lose it all, Rio. Just like I did.*

I clutch the photos and note against my chest, still on my knees as Rio barks out orders above me.

"Get him back here. Now! Call the men at the entrance. *Stop him from leaving.*"

"We have, Boss. They're waiting at the elevator bank downstairs."

More noise and a flurry of activity around me as some of my husband's goons race for the fire stairs. Others are speaking into mics, listening for responses and barking out orders.

"He's not there," someone says. Mitch? Lee? "The doors opened, and he wasn't in the fucking elevator car."

"*Lock this building down. And sweep it. Every fucking floor!*" That's Rio.

I can tell by that roar he's right on the edge of losing control.

I look up at him, silently begging him with my eyes. *Please don't let the darkness take you over. Not yet. Not till we make sure our daughter is safe.*

He bends and scoops me up in his arms, papers and all, and strides over to one of the couches in the VIP area. I don't even have time to register the fact that I didn't want to sit here where all the death came calling last time, before he sets me down beside him on the leather settee.

"Show me the note, Bianca."

I hand it over, and he reads quickly before crumpling the paper and throwing it across the room. It falls and rolls, landing up against the glass partition that surrounds this VIP space.

"We need to call the estate," I whisper. "Get Emilia down to the bunker. Get everyone down there."

There's a strange ringing in my ears that seems to warp the sound around me, making it almost nonexistent despite the number of people in the bar. As if I'm in a bubble.

*Maybe it's this bar*, I think, almost breaking into laughter. Every time I come here, something bad happens. I know it's shock making me feel this way, but that doesn't ease the strange feeling of being separated from reality.

And then a roar permeates the warped silence. Rio, letting out his emotions in a bone-shaking yell. Reality returns with the force of an explosion.

*"Get out!"* he screams. *"Everyone out. Now."*

It's testament to my level of shock that I don't even jump at the tone. Everyone else does, though. There's a rush of patrons and staff for the various exits, as if everyone in the club knows of Rio's reputation and is afraid he's lost it.

Minutes later, there's only us, and the goons, left.

I gently tug on his arm. "Could I use your cell, Rio? To call the nanny."

He fumbles in his jacket pocket and hands me his phone, before turning to someone and ordering them to call the man Danelli left in charge at the estate.

Penn answers after a couple of rings, sounding surprised to hear from me. "Everything all right, Mrs. Agosti?"

"Emilia. Is she..."

"She's fine, ma'am. She's been fed, bathed, and last I checked, which was less than two minutes ago, she was drifting off to sleep in her cot."

Relief floods through me, weakening my limbs. "Okay, good. Well, if Rio's men come up to see you, do exactly as they say. No questions asked."

I can hear her frown in her tone when she says, "Sure. Um, okay."

I hang up, feeling faintly better, though there's still the matter of what the man said...

*No. Don't think about that now.*

I turn to Rio and hand him back his phone. "I just spoke to Penn. Emilia's fine. She's—"

"Boss?" One of the goons has approached and interrupted me, which is unusual.

Rio and I both look at him, and my nerves kick straight back in again at the troubled expression on the man's face.

"I'm sorry, sir, but...we can't get through to the estate. No one there seems to be answering their phones. We've tried at least ten of the team."

"Try the rest. Call them all. My sister, too. Call Angel."

"Yes, sir. Already on it."

"But...I just spoke to Penn. The nanny," I clarify for the goon. "She's at the estate. She said Emilia is sleeping."

Rio stills, then slowly reaches for his phone and hands it back to me. "Call her back. And tell her to take Emilia and head straight down to the basement. She is not to wait for anyone."

Dread sends a shiver through me, and I punch in the number again with shaking fingers.

This time when the nanny answers, there's a strange note in her voice. "Ma'am? Something's wrong, isn't it? What's going on?"

"Penn, listen to me. Take Emilia now and head down to the bunker. Don't wait for security. Go now."

"All right. But we're fine here. I promise."

Rio grabs the phone from me. "Who's with you from the team?" He listens then says, "Put him on. Now."

Then he blinks and holds the phone away from his ear before letting out an expletive. "The call cut out."

The goon in front of us listens to his earpiece, then says, "Your sister is with Nikolas, sir, at his apartment in Seaport."

"That's something. Tell them to stay there. And get their security on alert. Tell them to keep watch for anything untoward."

"Will do, sir."

Rio jumps up from the couch, his hands clenched at his sides. "Take my wife upstairs to my suite and guard her with your life. And call my driver. And Danelli. I know he's coordinating the building search, but you're in charge of that now. Danelli's coming with me. We're heading back to the estate."

"Yes, sir."

"No way." I jump to my feet, too. "I am not going to be held upstairs while you... No. No *fucking* way, Rio."

"Bianca, this is not the time to—"

"*No*, Rio. She's my daughter. Yours, of course, but *mine* too. I'm going with you. No argument." I grin at him, aware there is no humor whatsoever in my expression. Rage is beginning to take over from my terror. How dare they threaten my daughter? "As you said, there's no *time* to argue."

The fact that he hesitates at all, let alone finally nods and starts barking out more orders, is testament to the stress he must be under. Nausea rolls through me, but I manage to hold it back. If I show the faintest sign of weakness right now, he will likely change his mind about taking me with him.

I am not going to be left behind. Not when it comes to Emilia.

## 25

*"Danger was the grindstone on which the swordsman whetted his spirit."*
Eiji Yoshikawa

*Bianca*

RIO MUST HAVE HAD an arsenal upstairs above the club because every man in our cavalcade on the return to the estate is armed to the hilt. More than they usually are. I've never seen so many weapons in one place, and my brain shies away from the fact that we may well be heading toward yet another violent bloodbath.

And this time, I volunteered to head right into the thick of it. But I don't have any choice. I can't leave my daughter's safety to a bunch of strangers to deal with.

I need to get back to my daughter. I need to make sure she's safe.

That's all I can focus on, and it becomes a mantra I repeat to myself over and over in the limo.

When we're almost home, Rio leans forward and presses a gun into my hands. I take it without protest, more because I'm too shocked at his expectation to even think of saying no.

I stare down at the black thing in my hand. The warmth of it sitting in my palms is unexpected. I always thought guns were made of metal, and holding one would feel cold in my grip. This isn't metal. It seems to be a hard plastic.

Why am I focusing on such mundane details? The fact is, I'm *holding a fucking gun*! And I'm unlikely to ever be able to point it at another human being, let alone pull the trigger.

*If it's a matter of life and death for Emilia*, a little voice whispers deep in my mind. Then *you'd do it.*

Then, and only then. Maybe.

"I don't know how to use a gun, Rio." I try to hand it back, but he waves his hands, forcing me to drop the thing back into my lap.

"I know you don't, little bird. That's something we may have to remedy in the future. But right now, I don't know what we are heading into, and I don't want you to be left helpless if there's an attack and we happen to get separated."

Hysteria threatens, and I'm proud of myself when I don't give in to it.

He grunts when I don't answer him, and then leans forward to point at different parts of the gun. "This is a Glock 19. The recoil if you need to fire it is not too bad, which is better for a beginner. The magazine has been loaded for you already. It has an inbuilt safety system, so you are less likely to blow off your foot."

"Oh."

"That was a joke, Bianca."

"Oh."

"A poor taste one, I can see. I was trying to lessen your tension. I apologize."

"Okay." I'm practically catatonic with stress. I can't even swallow properly as I don't think I have any saliva left. When I speak, my voice comes out all scratchy and rough. "Don't joke, please. Just... How do I... What..."

"Here." He taps different parts of the gun. "This is the grip. You should hold it with both hands. To load a bullet into the chamber, you pull this slide back and then release it. Do not put your finger here, on the trigger, unless you're ready to fire."

He talks me through it a little more, but I can barely concentrate. I have a loaded gun literally sitting in my lap, and I'm utterly terrified of it.

But I don't hand it back to him. Because what if I *do* need to protect myself or Emilia? I have no idea what the hell we're driving toward at the estate.

As we approach the gated entrance to our home, Rio's cell phone trills. He grabs it out quickly, and I see Danelli's name on the screen before he holds it up to his ear.

"Yes?"

I study his expression, my heart pounding. Is it more bad news? What's happening...

"Hmm. Have him meet us out front. I want to confirm it for myself."

He hangs up and reaches over to pat me gently on the knee. "Sounds like a false alarm. Danelli's men have made contact with all of those here at the estate. All is quiet here, apparently. No idea what happened earlier, but Danelli's team will secure the building while we wait at the front door."

"And Emilia?"

"I will have him fetch her up from the basement. I presume she is down there. And if she is still upstairs in the nursery, then we will replace the nanny because the instructions to her were made very clear."

"Okay." I still feel unsettled. Something isn't right.

And, judging by the tension still sharpening Rio's features, I suspect he feels the same sense of unease as me.

But it seems all really is quiet here. Danelli's Alpha and the Beta teams meet us beneath the portico at the front entrance, though Rio makes me wait in the vehicle until the all clear is given.

Everyone is accounted for. And when they check their phones, all have a signal. It is only then that Rio allows me to exit the limo.

Danelli steps up to stand in front of us. "Do you think it was an EMP, Boss? Though, maybe not. Wouldn't that have damaged their phones?"

"Possibly. Unless the pulse was small. But that wouldn't explain how Bianca managed to speak with the nanny. *Her* phone worked."

"True." Danelli frowns and then turns away for a moment, listening to something in his earpiece.

"Rio, what's an EMP?"

I feel like I'm getting a crash course in Rio's lifestyle. Mafia 101.

A small chuckle escapes me, and Rio raises a brow. Why do I always feel the need to laugh when my nerves are shot?

"Electromagnetic pulse," he explains calmly. "It can disable comms temporarily in a particular area."

"Oh." I frown. "But that would presumably take out *all* comms? Like Penn's phone too?"

"Indeed. So, therefore, unlikely to have been an EMP attack."

I open my mouth to ask another question, but Danelli lifts his head, and his face brightens with whatever he's just heard.

He shoots Rio the closest thing to a smile I've seen on the man's face. "They got the guy at the club, Boss. He was hiding on level four, in that section currently being renovated."

"Is he alive?"

"Yes. Want us to—"

"Extract the information you need first. Who he is. What he wants. And most importantly, who sent him there with those photographs and the threat."

My heart skips a beat at the realization I haven't yet told Rio what that man said to me in the club. I still need time to process what it means, but now I don't have that luxury. Especially if Rio's men are about to try and "extract" information…

"Are you going to kill him, Rio?"

His face shutters and his eyes are unreadable when he stares down at me. "Do you want me to answer you truthfully, Bianca?"

"That's a yes, then." My hand convulses, and I look down, shocked to realize I'm still holding on to the gun.

I don't even have anywhere to holster it. He gave me a gun but no holster. I chuckle again, feeling as if I may be losing my mind. If I haven't already lost it.

"My team will do what is required to get the information we need. So we can confirm who is behind this threat to our family and the business. And then we will stop the threat, once and for all. Is that not what you wish, too?"

"Of course. Only…" I have to tell him. "There's something I need to share with you about—"

"Boss?" Danelli is back in Rio's space, only this time there's no hint of a smile whatsoever on the *consigliere's* grim face.

Rio's gaze homes in on Danelli. "What?" he barks out.

"We can't find Emilia. Or the nanny. They're not down in the bunker, nor are they upstairs. Everyone else is fine, and there's no sign of any struggle, but there's no trace of your daughter, sir. None at all."

---

*"Courage is found in unlikely places."*
J.R.R. Tolkien

*Rio*

"Emilia's gone?" Bianca's voice squeaks out of her, barely there, and her face drains of color.

The distraction stops me from going into a full-blown meltdown. But only just. I grab her by the elbows as her legs begin to crumple and help her gently down onto the top step of the front entrance.

Then I sit beside her. "Breathe," I direct, pressing the back of her head down until it rests between her knees. "Just breathe. And keep your head down until you don't feel like you're about to faint anymore."

I stroke her hair, trying to keep my touch gentle despite the furnace of rage that has ignited inside me.

I look up over her head at my second. "That explains the comms, then. The woman wasn't here in the house when she took Bianca's call. So, chances are it *was* an EMP."

Danelli's eyes are stricken when he nods his agreement. He knows his team has failed me, and he knows there will be consequences for that failure. Out of everyone here, barring perhaps Bianca herself, Danelli understands my moods better than anyone. He knows my calm exterior is deceptive, and that the longer I hold everything in, the greater the explosion will be. It is only a matter of time.

But right this minute, Bianca needs me.

*Me*, not my inner monster. I wrestle the darkness back down into the box where it needs to stay. For now.

"Search the grounds," I tell him. "If it *was* a pulse, then it must have been small. Local. She may well have set it off herself on her way out."

"But the men at the gate confirmed they didn't see anyone leave…"

Danelli is right. And on the road in, we didn't pass anyone coming the other way. I don't believe she would have had that much of a head start. She likely thought she'd soothed our nerves when she reassured Bianca that every-thing was fine here.

I raise my head, my gut screaming at me with an undeni-able message. Time to listen.

"The river," I snap at my second. "There'll be a boat."

"But my men would have heard—"

"*Now*, Danelli. I don't believe she was expecting us to come home this early. She may still be down there…"

With my daughter. In the dark. By a deep and muddy river. I never give in to panic, but its tendrils squeeze at my heart.

It's cold tonight, but not raining or particularly windy. If Emilia is out there in the darkness, why can't I hear my daughter's cries on the gentle breeze that wafts in from the river?

What horror is the property search about to reveal?

"On it, Boss." My man races off into the darkness just as quickly as my thoughts head inward to my own darkness.

I return my focus back to Bianca. Holding on to what little light she can offer.

Slowly, she raises her head, blinking at me. There's some color in her cheeks once again. Not like the pastiness of a few minutes ago.

"Has the dizziness receded?"

She nods. "Yes. I'm not going to faint. Not now."

Without warning, she reaches up and cups my cheek. I haven't asked for comfort, but she must sense that I need it.

"We'll get her back, Rio."

We have to. I can't face the thought of any other scenario.

"We will." My vow thrums with conviction, but it is more for her sake, not for mine.

My life has not convinced me that happily ever after exists, and the fact that I've dared to aim for that, with Bianca and Emilia, has perhaps tempted the fates too much.

Happily ever after is never for the likes of me.

I take her hand from my cheek, press my lips to her palm, then return it to her lap, where she once again fastens her fingers around the Glock hanging between her legs. As if the gun is an actual lifeline, and she's clinging to it tightly.

"Now, I'm going to have two of my men accompany you down to the bunker, Bianca, and I don't want you to argue with—"

"No, Rio, wait. Don't send me away. Not yet. I have to—"

Shouts and yells break out in the darkness, coming from the direction of the river.

I lurch up and bark an order over my shoulder. "Don't you dare leave this house, Bianca. Go down to the bunker with..." I stare around wildly and spy her two regulars jogging back up the driveway from the direction of the gate. "Mitch and Leon. Go with them. And wait till I return."

Then I race off toward the yelling, drawing my gun from its holster and wondering if I'm about to discover my daughter alive.

Or dead.

---

### Bianca

*I HAVE to tell you about the guy at the club. About what he said to me when he handed me that envelope.*

I cannot get the words out in time, and Rio disappears as the night's darkness swallows him up.

I fling a glance at Mitch and Leon, who are heading my way with matching determined expressions, and then I slip off my heels and jump to my feet, racing after Rio in the direction of the men's yelling voices.

Grass and dampness squelch beneath my bare feet, but I don't stop. Has someone found Emilia? Why are they carrying on like that so much? Screaming and snarling like animals.

A shot rings out, and then another, and I screech in terror

and pump my legs even harder. I have to get there. I have to find my little girl...

I trip on something in the grass. A rock or an exposed tree root. Whatever it is, I go sprawling face-first into the dirt with the breath knocked out of me. I close my eyes and concentrate on getting my lungs to breathe again. When I open my eyes and look up, I recoil in horror at the sight before me.

Someone in the house must have switched on every single outdoor spotlight on the property. The darkness has disappeared, and the grassy landscape here, near the path ahead that leads down to the dock, is now illuminated in a bright golden glow that leaves nothing to the imagination.

I grope for my gun, pick it up, and clutch it close to my chest. I prefer the darkness to this terrifying tableau.

Men are fighting each other all across the grass, punches being thrown and bodies lunging and ducking as the thud of fists on flesh rings out. I can't even tell which of these are Rio's men. One of the spotlights catches on a knife, causing it to glint fiercely as the wielder raises his arm to strike.

Another shot rings out, and the knife-wielder drops to the ground. I don't think he was one of Rio's?

The action continues unabated. The gunshots haven't stopped any of them from trying to kill each other.

I start to raise my weapon but instantly lower it again. I don't even know who these people are or where my daughter is. If she's here at all?

What the fuck should I do? Where's Rio?

Mitch and Lee reach me then, and Lee drops to his knees beside me while Mitch rushes forward into the fray. "Ma'am, come on. We have to get you out of here."

He tugs at me, dragging me up to my feet. I wrench my arm out of his grip.

"No. Go help my husband," I command.

"Where…"

I wave my gun around. "In there somewhere. Go."

He turns in the direction I point, but pauses to take a deep breath. Then he races into the press of bodies and disappears from my view. Have I just sent Lee to his death? But where the hell is…

Oh. There he is. Rio is off to one side of the melee, and it looks like he's chasing after a small man who is heading into a scrub area along the bank of the river. It's…

My heart skips a beat. It's not a man. It's Penn, dressed in trousers and with her blonde hair mostly covered by a cap. I can't see Emilia anywhere. I start in their direction, staggering off to the side so I can skirt around the fighting men, and wincing when yet another gunshot releases. I'm still standing, still upright, so I guess it wasn't aimed at me.

I'm close enough to call out to Rio, only when I do and his shocked face whips around to me, so does Penn's. She turns and lifts…a gun? Does everyone have guns in this world? She aims it straight at my husband.

And then, as if the world has slowed and everything is warped, I hear the gun go off.

*Her* gun. Not mine. Not Rio's. Hers. And my husband staggers and then falls to the ground with a thud.

"No!" I scream, all the pent-up terror of the day rushing out of me in that desperate sound. I raise my gun and point it at her. "You shot him. You shot Rio Agosti. The man I love."

My gun wobbles in my hands and, far from looking afraid, she begins to laugh.

"Oh, Bianca. As if you would ever actually shoot another human being. We both know that."

She points her gun at me, still laughing, and part of me

wonders why she doesn't just shoot and get it over with. I blink at her, unable to process any thoughts in a coherent order. But then the most important question pops into my brain.

"Where's Emilia? Where's my daughter?"

I walk forward, feeling like I'm in some kind of daze, until I stand beside where Rio is lying in a pool of blood. I'm only a few feet away from the nanny. Her face should be so familiar, and yet, a stranger stares back at me.

"I want my daughter back, Penn. Where is she?"

"It's not what it seems, and you know why, Bianca. You were told."

What does that mean? "I trusted you. I thought you loved Emilia nearly as much as I do."

"I *did* care for her! I *do* care." She scowls at me, as if I've insulted her integrity. "You received that message at the club. You know you'll be reunited with your beloved daughter soon, if you cooperate. We'll be in touch with directions on how to get her back."

She turns to walk away, then swivels back when Rio makes an incoherent sound obviously born of pain. "But we don't need *him*."

She lifts the weapon toward Rio, cruel intent in her gaze, and I don't think anymore.

I just grit my teeth and pull the trigger.

My shoulders jerk, and I stagger back a step.

And my daughter's nanny drops her weapon and falls to the ground with a shocked gasp.

Rio scares me then, lurching up onto his hands and knees and crawling forward through the grass to grab Penn's gun and hold it.

I thought he was dead, or dying. Maybe he is. Maybe I've

lost all grip on reality.

Penn stares up at me from the ground, her mouth opening and closing and her eyes wide. "Wow." Her voice is a wet gurgle. "Didn't expect you to have the balls for *that*, girl."

She coughs, then keeps coughing, and my legs suddenly don't want to hold me up anymore.

I find myself on my knees, still clutching this *fucking gun*. I throw it to one side and lean forward, retching violently and bringing up everything in my stomach.

I barely even flinch when another *pop* sounds. Rio, finishing the job I started? I risk a glance up, then quickly look away.

Yep. He finished the job.

I keep my gaze averted from the result and begin to sob, hugging my stomach and wondering if I'm about to throw up again. There's nothing left in there. I *can't* throw up again.

How has this happened? How in a million fucking *years* has this happened? I have just become one of them. A monster. A murderer.

A Mafia princess with blood on my hands and the darkest of empty places where my heart used to be.

Just like Rio. Only far, far worse. Because Rio was born to this life, raised in it, and has never known anything different. In many ways, he's never had a choice regarding his path in life.

Unlike me. I knew different. I knew better, and I've sure as hell had options that didn't lead here.

But the choices I've made have led to this. And for what? For *nothing*.

Because I still don't have my beautiful daughter back.

And now, I've given up everything. Including my morality.

"*Integrity is telling myself the truth. And honesty is telling the truth to other people.*"
Spencer Johnson

*Bianca*

Rɪᴏ's labored breathing breaks through my growing hysteria, and I come back to reality with a burst of adrenaline that spikes my heart rate.

He was shot. How could I forget that? My husband was *shot,* and I need to get him help.

I need to be strong now. Not weak.

I have to be a proper mob boss's wife, and I need to step up and help him in his moment of need, even if I want to run as fast as I can from this place of destruction.

*You did help him already*, my mind whispers. *You* shot *someone for him.*

I stagger up to my feet, away from the putrid pile of vomit on the ground. I studiously ignore Pe—*no, don't give her a name*, my mind screams at me. I ignore the *female body* sprawled in the dirt, and make my way over to where Rio ended up when he crawled to grab the female's weapon.

He's swaying on his knees, and his normally tanned face has a pale, sweaty sheen.

"Lie down," I say between gasps, realizing I need to slow my breathing. I'm likely going to hyperventilate if I don't. "Where did she get you, Rio? What can I do?"

I start patting him all over, looking for the wound, but he bats my exploring hands away before releasing a tiny chuckle. The sound is followed by a moan.

"Jesus. Okay, no laughing." His voice is raspy, but then he adds, "I'm fine, *mia cara*. Well, I'm not, but I will be."

"But she shot you."

"Indeed. Here." He half lifts an arm and peers down at his ribs on the left side, and I shriek when I see how much blood soaks his clothing.

"Oh my God!" This time when I reach for his shirt, I try to be gentle, and he doesn't bat me away. I lift the shirt carefully to reveal torn flesh beneath. "I don't know what to do to help you," I say. "Please, tell me what to do. Should I put pressure on it? Go for help?"

*I can't lose you* and *Emilia tonight*. I don't express the fear out loud, but it is as if he knows the way my brain works and guesses anyway.

"You won't lose me, Bianca. And take heart from what she said." He jerks his head in the female's direction. "Emilia is alive and safe. For now."

"But your chest…"

"The bullet hit a rib and seems to have deflected along the

bone. It hasn't gone in, I don't think. Hurts like a mother-fucking bitch, though."

When Rio curses, it is usually in Italian. To hear the matter-of-fact way in which he delivers the English swear words sounds so wrong coming out of his mouth.

"Can you walk? I need to get you to help. I can support you, if you can walk a bit?"

I unbutton his shirt and slide it off, bunching it up and pressing it gently against his wound. He hisses a little, but then laughs lightly. Then winces, as if he can't decide whether to give in to the pain or not.

"You will have to learn to wear dark clothes in this world, little bird, like me." He gestures to the shirt, which is black. "That beautiful cream dress of yours is already half ruined with blood and mud. But I fear I'm a little too heavy for you. I will just do as you say, I think, and lie down here for a bit."

He starts to drop, and thank God he's only on his knees because, somehow, I'm able to brace his fall, at least a little, and ease him down onto the grass. His face has turned even grayer than before, and his eyelids flutter as if he wants to fall asleep. The bullet may have only grazed him, but he's obviously lost a lot of blood, and no doubt shock is setting in.

"I'll get help, Rio. I'll be quick."

I jump to my feet and rush back up the path through the trees, toward where the fight was happening earlier. I can't hear any more yelling or scuffling, only muffled conversation, so I assume the fight must be over. I pray Rio's side won because I can't move him on my own, and I don't know who I'm about to find up ahead.

I burst out of the trees and stop short at the sight of about thirty men all raising their guns in my direction at once.

"Jesus fucking Christ. Bianca!" That voice is Danelli's.

He survived. Which means Rio's side must have won. He hurries forward, his horrified gaze on my blood-soaked dress. "You nearly got yourself shot just then, woman. Are you injured? Were you shot?"

I stagger closer, seeing Lee and Mitch among the men pulling dead bodies into two piles. Ours and theirs? Thank goodness my two goons survived. Only one of the Leons has died on my watch, then.

I turn back to Danelli. "It's not my blood. It's Rio's. Penn shot him," I explain. "And then I shot Penn. And then Rio shot Penn. And now she's damn well dead. Really fucking dead."

I want to burst into tears but, somehow, only laughter emerges. Danelli's free hand comes up and makes the sign of the cross.

I'm not sure if the sign is for Rio. Or because he thinks I've become a madwoman and he's seeking divine protection. The thought stops my laughter more effectively than a slap to the face.

*Time for hysterics later. Focus, Bianca. Focus.*

"Rio's alive, Danelli. He needs help. Please. I can't carry him on my own." I point back down the trail. "That way. Not far. He lost a lot of blood."

---

*Rio*

MY MEMORY of how I got back to the house is a little hazy. I think several of Danelli's team may have carried me here. Our doctor is already waiting for me in my first-floor sitting room, apparently having received a call from one of the team.

I have no idea what he was doing when he was summoned, nor do I care, but he must have been close by. He is on retainer, and as such, we own him.

While we have used him many times in the past, I have not had a reason to call him in for me before now.

Once he gets my wound cleaned and stitched up, given me some fluids and injected me with antibiotics, I start to think more clearly.

I look around for Bianca but can't see her anywhere. "Where is my wife?"

Danelli steps forward. "Mrs. Agosti was covered in blood. She wanted to shower and change. I think she was also a little…"

"Hysterical?"

"Yeah." My second scrunches his face. "It's been a long time for me, but I'm sure everyone here remembers their first kill."

A brief silence falls among those in the room, and I'm instantly transported back to that day my father made me kill my first at the age of thirteen. It was indeed long ago, but the effect of it is still with me today.

I don't want that darkness for Bianca. She's supposed to be my source of light.

Then the silence is broken by the doctor, who gently coughs.

"Yes?" I bark out.

"I'll give you an injection now for the pain, Mr. Agosti."

"No."

"But—"

"I said no. I need a clear head. Can you guarantee that"— I point to the syringe in his hand—"will leave my head clear?"

"I, well, no, it won't. It will put you to sleep, most likely."

"Then no. I am not going to drift off to sleep while my *fucking daughter is missing*!"

The doctor backs away quickly. "Sorry, sir. I'll just..."

He scurries over to pack up his equipment. I take a deep breath, which I instantly regret, only just managing to hold in the groan. Pain relief may be enticing, especially with the agony in my side every time I breathe or adjust my position. But the pain will pass. And every minute wasted is time that could be spent locating Emilia.

"I will at least leave these here for you. You *will* need them to sleep, Mr. Agosti," he murmurs, and places a pack of pain pills on the mantel above the fireplace. "I will return tomorrow to check the wound and change the dressing. Any sign of redness or if you develop a fever, you must call me back immediately. Do you understand?"

"I do. I will be fine."

"You will have a scar," he says drily.

"I don't care about that."

I care that my daughter is missing, and I care that my wife isn't here by my side. Not for my sake, but for hers. I know Bianca. She'll be drowning in a vat of guilt right now. She has no need to feel that way because she didn't fire the killing shot. I did.

But that won't change the fact that she'll be wrestling with what she's done.

The fact is, Bianca showed incredible bravery tonight. If she hadn't shot Emilia's nanny when she did, the simple fact is I would not have survived.

My wife saved my life. In return, I will offer her my strength so she can get through this nightmare and come out the other side without fragmenting into a million tiny pieces.

Or sinking into the darkness that took me so many years ago.

"Fetch Bianca here, now."

Someone rushes out to do my bidding, and while I wait for her to be brought to me, I turn to face my second, who has been standing at attention near the fireplace, waiting for the doctor to finish.

"Talk to me, Danelli. What do you have?"

"There were twenty-five men, in addition to the nanny. It looks like the men came in by river and were only meant to be there as backup if the nanny didn't succeed in handing over your..." He clears his throat, then finishes, "Your daughter to whoever was waiting on the boat. When some of my team saw the boat leaving the dock, they rushed down there, and this band of men provided a distraction. In the confusion, the boat got away. I'm sorry, Boss."

Sorry. He's *sorry*? My mouth presses together so tightly I fear I may crack my jaw. "Which direction did it head?"

"Downriver. Toward the wharf."

Of course it did. Upriver would have been easier to trace. "And how many of them are now dead?"

"Seventeen, Boss. Unfortunately, they got nine of ours."

My heart sinks. *Nine*. That's a lot of families who will be grieving tomorrow. I will send someone around to each family, of course, to deliver the news and offer support from the Agosti family. But that won't soften the blow of finding out a loved one has been gunned down in the line of duty. Nothing can soften that news.

"And do we know any more about who sent them? Surely, some of these men look familiar to *someone*. We have seventeen dead bodies from someone else's crew out there on my grounds. Spread the word. I want information, and I want it *now*. Offer a reward for the information. One million dollars."

Danelli's mouth drops open. "A million?"

I spear him with an unblinking stare. "It *is* my daughter, Danelli. If nothing is forthcoming in the first twelve hours, up the reward to two million."

"Yes, sir." He almost salutes. I see his fingers itching to do so. Instead, he clenches his hands into fists. "I have people going through the pockets as we speak. Taking photos of their faces. We'll put the word out. With this many men, someone will know. And with that level of reward...it's only a matter of time before we discover which crew they're from, Boss."

I agree with his assessment. Someone will talk, and soon. At least one of those dead men will be recognized by someone.

Whoever is in charge of these sustained attacks has just made a soon-to-be-fatal error.

*"Not until we are lost do we begin to understand ourselves."*
Henry David Thoreau

*Bianca*

I STRIP off the bloodied clothing as soon as I reach the bedroom and reopen the door to throw them out into the hallway. I don't care that Lee, stationed outside, may have just caught a glimpse of my nakedness. I cannot bear the thought of those clothes anywhere in this space. Even in the washing hamper. Or in the trash.

"Burn them," I call out through the door.

"Will do, ma'am," comes the muffled response.

I turn the shower on and make the water as hot as I can stand. Then I wash my hair and scrub and scrub my body for what feels like hours. But I can't seem to get clean. Eventually, I sink down onto the tiled floor and put my head onto my bent knees, letting the water wash over my shoulder blades and allowing the tears to fall.

I killed a woman. Well, technically Rio did, but I was instrumental in her death.

Not just anyone. A woman I *knew*. A woman I trusted enough to leave my child in her care.

Penn was *nice*. She cared about Emilia—or at least, she appeared to—almost as much as I did. I can't process the fact that she's actually dead, and that I was the one who caused her death.

I keep seeing her face, over and over, even when I squeeze my eyes shut. There's a hollow, empty feeling in my chest, like the act of killing her somehow snuffed out the life in my own heart. How does Rio live with this? How do any of them live with this empty ache inside?

I don't know if I'll ever be able to fall asleep again.

And above and beyond everything else I'm feeling about Penn's death, I'm terrified for my baby. Emilia is gone. Taken by God knows who, for God knows what purpose, and who knows if I'll ever get my innocent little girl back.

Is she afraid of whoever took her? Are they treating her okay? Feeding her the right kind of food? Changing her diaper regularly? Do they even know how to look after a six-month-old child? What if she wants her momma, as she calls me, or her dadda? And neither of us comes when she cries out? Will she feel abandoned by the ones who are supposed to love and protect her?

If we get her back, will she remember this incident? Will it traumatize her forever?

The only faint hope I try to cling to is that she's the same age now that I was when I was whisked away by *my* nanny and dumped on the steps of a church, and I honestly don't remember any of that.

Hopefully, if—no, I correct myself, *when*—she's back in my arms, safe and sound, she won't remember a thing about it.

As I sit here, hot water pouring down over my body, something about my thoughts begins to jar. Slowly, I lift my head.

*Taken by God knows who.*

But that isn't correct. I *do* know who took her. Or at least, I think I do. Remembering what Penn said before she died, and how she alluded to the guy in the club, the suspicion crystallizes into a certainty.

I stagger to my feet and shut off the water, then grab a fluffy white towel and dry off as quickly as I can. I have to get downstairs and speak with Rio. Even if he's not well enough to do anything right now, I have to tell him what the man said to me in the club.

And then, together, we will uncover the truth about our enemy. And go get our daughter back.

If it's not already too late to save her.

---

*Rio*

WHEN BIANCA ENTERS the sitting room, a waft of her sweet citrus scent accompanies her. Her skin is pink and clean-looking, and her hair still damp. She's wearing a black sweater and casual black sweatpants, and she looks as beautiful and innocent as ever.

But as she comes close, I notice subtle differences in her

demeanor. The tension in her jaw, the rigid line of her shoulders, and worst of all, an empty darkness behind her eyes that I've never seen there before.

It matches what I see in the mirror every morning when I stare at my own reflection. I never want to see that in my wife, and yet there it is, right in front of me.

Pity rises in my chest for the mental journey I know she has ahead of her. But no matter how hard it is, I will not do to her what my mother did to me. I will never tell her to lock the darkness away, because when you do that, it only grows.

I will get her the help she needs to deal with the trauma of killing someone. If she wants it.

But not until we get our daughter back.

She squats down beside me and strokes a gentle hand over my thigh, and I have to fight not to fold her into my arms and command her to stay there forever.

Instead, I cover her hand with mine, taking a moment to simply enjoy the connection, skin to skin.

"Are you feeling all right, Rio? What did the doctor say?" Her voice is surprisingly strong.

I half expected her to be crying and trembling, but she isn't showing any of the angst I know must be eating her up deep down inside.

"I'm fine, *mia cara.* All stitched up and almost as good as new. Are *you*…all right?"

Ah, there it is, finally. The brief tremble of her mouth, the jolt of her pulse beneath my fingers as I caress her wrist.

But then she lifts her lips into an obviously fake smile and raises her chin to meet my gaze. "Of course. I'm fine. I didn't get…shot."

"Bianca, we will talk about what happened out there in the forest—"

"No. I don't want to. Not now." She snatches her hand back from beneath mine and rubs her palms together.

I open my mouth to say something else, but she shakes her head, stalling my words.

"Rio, wait. There's something I need to tell you. I have information that I think you need to hear. I... I would have told you earlier, but this whole night has been... Well."

She swallows, and her eyes dart around nervously. She is not all right. Not by a long shot.

I pat the seat beside me on my uninjured side, and she climbs up and slides onto it. I wrap my right arm around her shoulders, securing her against me, and she lets out a long sigh as if my touch has given her comfort.

"Rio, please don't be mad at me. I wanted to tell you... I tried a few times to tell you..."

My senses instantly go on alert. Somehow, I know this is going to be momentous.

"What is it, Bianca? The nanny alluded to something out there. She said you were told. In the club. Is that what you want to talk to me about?"

She nods, and keeps nodding, as if her nerves have gotten the better of her.

I take her chin between my thumb and forefinger and bring her nod to an end. "What did the man say to you, Bianca?"

Her body begins to shake. She clutches her hands in her lap. "He said... He said... It's so crazy, and it can't be real. I'm sure of it. But Rio, he said my mother, Rina..."

Suddenly, she breaks out of my hold and jumps to her feet. She turns to face me, and her eyes flash with unreadable emotion. Her voice is loud in the room as the words rush out of her.

"He said my mother, Rina Carlotti, somehow survived the car bomb that supposedly killed her. He said my mother is still alive."

I blink at her in shock, unable to formulate words.

She sucks in a breath and lets it out in a hiss before repeating the shocking allegation.

"Rio, I think my *birth mother* is still alive, and I think she's the one behind all these attacks."

*"Once you eliminate the impossible, whatever remains, no matter how improbable, must be the truth."*
Arthur Conan Doyle

*Bianca*

RIO'S HEAD reels back as if I've slapped his cheek. Then the familiar mask drops over his features, and his expression turns inscrutable.

In the past, whenever I saw that expression, I assumed it's because he's cold. Emotionless. A monster.

But now I know better. A tiny tic beneath his left eye starts up, betraying him. He's not emotionless. He's fuming with rage, and terrified for our daughter, just as much as I am, only he's trying to hide his reaction from me and everyone else.

"That's impossible," he says at last.

His tone is stiff, formal. Obviously, he doesn't believe what I've said can be true.

I know how he feels. I can scarcely believe it either.

But the more I think about it, the more I feel like it fits. Penn wasn't afraid for Emilia, and not because she was simply a coldhearted kidnapping bitch. She wasn't afraid because she didn't feel like she needed to be. She knew that whoever has our daughter doesn't want to harm her.

And who else would have Emilia's best interests at heart? Her grandmother.

"I know you don't believe me, but—"

"There was DNA evidence at the scene, Bianca. DNA that matched both your mother and your father. Witnesses saw them both get into the vehicle, and afterwards, well, by all accounts, no one could survive a blast like that."

I can't stay still. I feel like ants are crawling all over my body. I need to do something. Move. Something. I begin to pace up and back in front of the fireplace, my toes curling into the plush rug as I move.

Suddenly, I stop and poke a finger his way. "And you've never faked a death before? Set up a scene to look like one thing when it really is another? Paid off witnesses? Rigged DNA evidence?"

"I…"

"Thought so."

He can't deny it. I see the truth in his eyes.

"It's not impossible," he says in a slow, considered tone. "But it really is improbable. Do you not think your mother would have reached out to you at some point in the past twenty-six years if she were alive?"

"Maybe she didn't want to risk putting me in danger."

"Well, she's certainly doing the opposite now. If it really is her."

I stop pacing and turn to look at the flames in the grate. He's right. All her actions *are* putting us in danger now. Me, Emilia, and Rio. Why would she do that?

And if she did want the Carlotti business back again, then why not simply come forward when word got out that Rio had found me and planned to marry me? For that matter, why not come forward all those years ago after my birth father died?

Part of me wants it to be true. Desperately. If she *is* alive, then maybe one day I can meet her, and truly have a chance to understand who I am and what my heritage is. Emilia could have the chance to know and understand *her* heritage, too.

But maybe Rio is right after all. Maybe I'm just clutching at nonexistent straws.

The kernel of hope that flared to life when the man whispered those words in my ear snuffs out, and my shoulders slump. I grab the edge of the mantel and lean my forehead against the polished wood.

"Then we're back to square one again. With nothing. No clue as to who has Emilia, or why."

Tears burn my eyes, and I blink them back, refusing to let them fall. Then Rio's warm body presses against my back, and I turn and lean my head against his chest.

"We are not at square one. We have a lot more now than we had this morning. Or"—he glances at the clock on the mantel—"yesterday morning."

"Like what?"

"Like seventeen dead bodies out there who worked for someone in the industry. And when we identify who, we'll have them. We also have the message about your mother, which may or may not be true. But we can confirm that one way or the other, as I believe my men still have the man locked up at the club. We have Penn, who…"

He stops short, and when I look up at him to see what's wrong, his face has twisted into such a mask of rage that I almost whimper when I see it.

"What, Rio? You're scaring me all of a sudden."

"Penn," he says, and nods. "Yes. It all makes sense now."

"What do you mean?"

Rio steps back from me, and now it is his turn to pace back and forth along the rug. At the rate we're going, we'll need a new rug by morning. "All along I thought it was Martelli, angling for entry into the Boston area. If not him, then I was looking at Darov as a possible second option."

"Me too," I say, still not sure where this is headed. "Well, not Darov. But Martelli, yes. I almost asked him that night if he had someone named Antonio working for him."

Rio snorts, then winces. "I am very glad you did not do that, Bianca. Martelli would have taken that as a highly offensive slap in the face and, as you know, he does not respond well to perceived slights."

"But you're saying it wasn't him? Then who…"

Even before he continues, realization dawns in my gut.

"No." I clutch at my chest, having to force myself to keep breathing. "Not *Rossi*. Surely not Carlos Rossi."

"Yes," Rio says. "It's the only explanation that fits. There is one person who has been at the center of everything since the beginning. He knew my parents, and yours. He was in love with your mother, Bianca. He hid you away and gave me the name Antonio, sending all the families heading out on various wild goose chases. Pitting us against each other with innuendo and suspicion, and then sliding in to sabotage things where he could. He even gave me…"

"What, Rio? What did he give you?"

"He gave me Penn, Bianca. He gave me a referral for a nanny, and it led me straight to Penn."

"But it can't be true. Why…"

Rio's lips twist into a parody of a smile. But his eyes burn like black holes in his face, and even though I know his rage isn't directed at me, I stumble back a step, almost into the fireplace.

"Your mother, of course," Rio says.

He reaches out and pulls me back from the fireplace in an almost absent-minded fashion. I stagger over to the couch and sink down on it, hunching into myself to try and seem smaller.

His inner monster is coming to life before my very eyes.

"Rina *is* alive," he grates out. "She must be. And Carlos Rossi is working with her to bring us all down and take over everything. For her."

---

I HOPE you enjoyed book two of the *Dark Enemies* trilogy. The series concludes in book three, *Ruthless Enemy*.

# RUTHLESS ENEMY

## DARK ENEMIES BOOK THREE

**Blurb**

**I was innocent, until the Mafia crime lord kidnapped me and forced me to marry him.**

Now there is blood on my hands and guilt in my heart, and the stakes have never been higher.

But Rio—my kidnapper, my husband, my lover—is the only one I can trust to bring down our common enemy who has taken everything I've ever held dear.

And the impossible choice I now have to make, means someone I love, is going to die.

The thrilling conclusion to the deliciously dangerous *Dark Enemies* trilogy featuring Rio Agosti and Bianca Carlotti. No cliffhanger!

# ABOUT THE AUTHOR

Zoe Delaney is the dark contemporary romantic suspense pen name of *USA Today* bestselling author, Jen Katemi.

When Zoe isn't writing, she runs an editing and proof-reading business, dotes on her daughters and pampers various cats—including a rescue with one hip. She lives in Melbourne, Australia.

Find out more or sign up for her reader newsletter at her website and never miss a new release:

www.Zoe-Delaney.com

BOOKS BY ZOE DELANEY

**Dark Enemies series**
Ruthless Possession
Ruthless Betrayal
Ruthless Enemy

**Dark Vows series**
Reckless Heir
Reckless King
Reckless Vow

www.ingramcontent.com/pod-product-compliance
Lightning Source LLC
Chambersburg PA
CBHW031947240626
47153CB00003B/887